First Aid for Fairies
and Other Fabled Beasts

FABLED BEAST CHRONICLES

First Aid for Fairies
and Other Fabled Beasts

LARI DON

 Kelpies

Kelpies is an imprint of Floris Books

First published in 2008 by Floris Books
This new edition published in 2014

The publisher acknowledges subsidy from Creative
Scotland towards the publication of this volume

Cover font designed by Juan Casco
www.juancasco.net

 This book is also available
as an eBook

British Library CIP Data available
ISBN 978-178250-137-4
Printed in Great Britain
by DS Smith Print Solutions, Glasgow

To Mirren and Gowan

Thanks for playing with the tiny pony
and the shell

Chapter 1

Clip clop clip scrape.
Clip clop clip scrape.

The slow hoofbeats moved up the dark lane to the vet's house and surgery.

Clip clop clip scrape.
Clip clop clip scrape.

The boy's breath made clouds in the air, and he gasped with pain every time the fourth hoof touched the ground.

Clip clop clip scrape.
Clip clop clip scrape.

Helen closed her diary after another entry of school, violin practice, tea and homework. She wondered whether she should just write "same as yesterday," as she had done nothing new for weeks. Like yesterday, she still hadn't found the perfect tune, so she hadn't been able to practise the most important piece of music. She sighed. There was only a week left to go until the concert.

She put the diary up high where Nicola couldn't reach to scribble on it, and went to the window to close the blind. She saw a shape moving up the lane. A horse? She opened her window a little.

Clip clop clip scrape.
Clip clop clip scrape.

The horse looked odd. It was limping, the rider was leaning too far forward over the horse's neck, and she couldn't see the horse's head. It must be hanging down very low. Yet the horse struggled up the lane.

Clip clop clip scrape.
Clip clop clip scrape.

Mum wouldn't be pleased if this was a late patient. She'd been out all evening with a flock of sheep that had run into a barbed wire fence after being panicked by a strange dog. Now she was soaking in a hot bubbly bath with a book and some biscuits. And Dad wouldn't be pleased if the doorbell woke Nicola, he was trying to get some urgent work done on the computer.

If it was just a local rider and a pony with a stone in

its hoof, Helen could give them a hoof pick and a torch and they could sort themselves out.

She crept downstairs and grabbed her fleece and her wellies, hoping to get out into the garden before the rider rang the doorbell and disturbed everyone else.

Helen opened the front door as fast as she could, still waggling her feet into her boots. "Hold on a minute," she whispered.

Just before she pulled her fleece over her head, she saw a bare-chested boy on a chestnut horse, standing in the front garden.

No. He wasn't on the horse ... he *was* the horse!

The boy and the horse seemed to melt into each other.

Helen stopped for a moment with the red fleece over her face. She shook her head, yanked the fleece down to her shoulders and looked again.

The boy had a horse's legs, back and tail.

The horse had a boy's head, arms and chest.

The boy's head said clearly, "Are you the horse healer? Can you heal me?" He pointed to the horse's back leg, which was bleeding from a deep open gash.

Helen looked behind her. No one in the house seemed to have heard.

"Shhhh," she said. She put her arms through the sleeves of her fleece, grabbed the bunch of keys from behind the door, and stepped out into the garden.

Without saying another word, because she couldn't think of any sensible ones, Helen led the lame horse-boy to the large animal surgery by the side of the house.

She unlocked the sliding doors, put the lights on, and ushered him in. He squinted at the bright light shining off the white cupboards and the gleaming metal equipment, then he limped inside. His hooves were loud on the concrete floor.

"Shhhh!"

Helen looked at him, seeing him properly for the first time now they were out of the night. But even in the clear clean light, she couldn't understand what she saw.

She remembered what men's torsos on horses' bodies were called. *Centaurs.* But that was a mythological name for a fantastic animal. They weren't real. She doubted they'd even existed in ancient Greece, let alone in the south of Scotland in the twenty-first century.

"You're a centaur."

"Yes. You're a horse healer. Kindly heal my leg."

"I'm not a horse healer. My Mum is the vet."

"Then fetch her ..."

A gust of freezing winter wind blew in through the door, and Helen turned to close it. As the door started to slide shut, the creature crouching in the bush just three steps away grunted with frustration. Now he couldn't see the centaur or the girl with the curly black hair. Should he wait here until the colt came out, or go back now and tell his Master that the young fool had involved a human child? Helen shoved the door until it clicked closed. She shouldn't have taken a stranger into her Mum's surgery, and she didn't want anyone to see the light.

She turned back to the centaur in the middle of the floor. "My Mum doesn't believe in centaurs or cyclops or sirens or anything like that. She only believes in science books. If she doesn't believe in you, she can't really bandage you up."

"Do you believe in me?"

Helen examined him from a distance. He scowled back at her.

The glossy horsehair on his horse body seemed to grow from the same skin as his boy's tummy and back. The tangled hair on his boy's head was the same reddish colour as the horsehair. Most of the hair on his head was hanging long onto his shoulders, but some was tied up off his face in a small ponytail above his forehead. She noticed scrapes and bruises on his bare skin. The horse and the boy had both been injured recently.

"Do you believe in me?" he demanded again.

He didn't look like a circus trick. He wasn't half a pantomime horse. But there was only one way to be sure.

Helen was used to boys in the playground and horses in the fields and she wasn't afraid of either. This horse-boy shouldn't frighten her.

So she took a step forward. She reached out her hand and ran it from his boy's back to his horse's flank. He hunched his shoulders, clearly annoyed at being touched, but he didn't shy away. The boy's skin was warm, and so was the horse's hair. There were no joins.

"Yes, I believe in you."

"Then you can bandage me."

"No, I can't. I'm not a vet. You have to study for years at university to be a vet. I'm not even at the high school yet."

"Hasn't your mother passed her skills and knowledge down to you? Don't you watch and learn from your elders?"

Helen knew how to wipe dog hairs off the table in

the small animal surgery in the house, and how to clean horse droppings off this concrete floor. She knew how to take messages from farmers about lambing and how to spell the names of the most common worming pills. But she didn't really want to know any more.

All her friends thought it was so cool having a Mum who was a vet – cute kittens, pretty puppies – but Helen saw the bitten fingers and the stinking overalls, and heard the stories about putting old pets out of their misery. She didn't want to be a vet. She wanted to be a musician. She wanted to work in a nice warm theatre or studio. Perhaps the occasional outdoor performance, in the summer. No mud or blood or dung.

"No. I'm not learning her skills and knowledge. I'm learning my own. I'm not a healer. I'm a musician."

The boy closed his eyes and sighed.

He was much taller than Helen, because his horse legs were longer than her human legs. But with his scowling eyes closed, and his confident voice quiet, he didn't seem much older than her. Suddenly he looked sad and in pain.

He opened his eyes again.

"What can I do, healer's child?"

She looked at his leg. It was dripping blood all over the floor. At least she was qualified to clean the floor, but perhaps she could have a go at cleaning the leg too.

"Stand there."

She went over to her Mum's supplies. She often tidied them in exchange for pocket money, so she knew where most things were.

Helen gathered big antiseptic swabs, horse bandages and a bottle of pink antiseptic solution. She pulled a low stool over to the boy's back legs.

Then she thought, what would Mum do? First she would take notes. So she pulled a new notebook from the desk and asked, "What's your name and how did this injury occur?"

"I am Yann. And it's none of your business how I hurt myself."

"Yes, it is. If I'm going to fix you, I need to know what hurt you."

"I cut myself jumping over a wall," he muttered.

"Was the wall too high for you?"

"No wall is too high! I misjudged it a little. I was distracted."

Helen grinned. She recognized the excuses boys at school made when they missed an easy shot at goal.

"I'm just going to wipe the dirt out of the wound, then put a covering on to keep it clean. It might sting a bit. Try to stay still."

"I am not afraid of pain."

"Well, aren't you brave. But if you aren't a little bit afraid of pain, you'll just keep damaging yourself."

Yann snorted, but didn't answer her.

Helen tore open a packet of swabs, soaked one in antiseptic and started to clear away the blood. She had hoped that once the blood was cleaned up, the wound would be quite small. But it ran right from his hoof, past his fetlock, up to his hock, and then curved round in a jagged edge. His lower leg had been ripped open and a flap of skin was hanging off.

He hissed and one of his front hooves scraped the floor jerkily as she cleaned under the flap. But his back leg stayed still.

"You're doing really well. Just a little bit more." She

recognised the sing song voice her Mum used to calm animals.

She gently cleaned blood, hairs and dirt out of the cut, and dropped the swabs on the floor.

She examined the clean wound.

"I can't just bandage you. I think this needs stitches."

"Go on then. I won't move."

"But I can't do stitches. I need to go and get my Mum."

"But you said she won't believe in me."

"She'll believe in the wound, Yann. She'll fix your leg before she worries about your top half."

"Then what will she do?"

Helen shrugged. "She'll either think she's dreaming, or she'll call the police. But I'm sure she would stitch you up first."

"What's the police?"

"They arrest people who've broken the law."

"I have not broken any of *your* laws," Yann insisted.

"You'll be fine then. But no adult is going to let you gallop off. They'll want to know what you are and where you came from."

"That is no one's business but my own. Can you sew?"

"Yes, and knit and weave and crochet and I can sing all fifteen verses of ..."

"If you can sew, you can stitch me up. I would be very obliged if you would do so."

"Don't you have centaur doctors, where you come from?' Helen asked. 'Couldn't you get them to fix you?"

"I can't tell ... It's none of your business. I have asked for your help, and by all the laws of hospitality you should give me that help."

"You're being far too rude to expect any hospitality."

"I shall make a bargain with you, healer's child. If you heal me, I promise to grant you a wish."

"Okay. I wish you would tell me what's going on ..."

"Oh no, I mean a tooth fairy type wish: a vision of your future husband, or a puppy for your birthday or something."

Helen laughed. "I don't want a husband, and we get far too many puppies here as it is. Let me do what I can with your leg, and then we'll see."

She reached up to the shelves to find the suturing equipment: a sterile needle, strong dissolving suturing thread, forceps and finally, right at the back, the metal needle holders shaped like skinny scissors.

When she had first shown an interest in making clothes for her toys, her Mum had let her practise not just with ordinary needles and thread, but also with fancy, curved suturing needles. Helen remembered that she had used the forceps to hold the edges of the material together, and the needle holder to push the needle through, so that her fingers didn't actually touch the needle. But suturing needles hadn't been much use for making teddy bears' pyjamas, so she hadn't used them for years.

Sewing up the wound in Yann's leg was nothing like stitching felt or cotton. It was more like sewing leather or plastic. She had to force the needle through with all her strength, then tug the thread after it to hold the skin together.

Yann didn't move, but she could hear his breathing. He took a deep breath as she picked up the edges of the skin with the forceps, held his breath as she forced the needle through, and didn't let it out until she had finished tugging. She glanced up after she had tied off the seventh stitch. He had one hand over his eyes.

"I'm nearly done. I'm sorry it hurts."

He didn't answer. He just kept breathing. Helen kept sewing.

Finally, she knotted the last stitch and checked along the length of the wound. The stitches were uneven, but the wound met all the way round, which she thought was the important thing.

"That's me done. Here, wipe the sweat off your forehead."

She handed him a hanky and turned her back for a moment, placing the used needle carefully in the yellow bin with the orange lid.

When she turned back, there were no tears on his face. It wasn't her business if there ever had been.

Helen said gently, "Please get someone older to look at it when you get home. The way I've done it, there might be a scar."

"If so, it will be a scar honourably won. Your stitches will be all I need. Thank you. I will leave now."

"Hold on. I have to cover it up. And you have to tell me your story of the high wall and the distraction and why you can't tell your own doctors."

"There is nothing to tell. Just a foolish accident."

"And the teeth?"

"What teeth?"

She bent down and took a couple of small white objects from the heap of bloody swabs on the floor.

"These teeth. They were stuck in the wound."

His eyes brightened.

"May I have those? It is always useful to have a tooth of the creature that bit you."

"Not yet." She slipped the sharp teeth into her jeans pocket, and picked up the horse bandages.

She held a sterile pad over the wound and wrapped a soft white bandage round it, winding upwards from his hoof. Then, she fastened everything neatly and securely with wide sticky tape. She stood up and looked at her handiwork. She was fairly sure it wouldn't unravel or slip off.

"How does that feel?"

"It feels strong. I thank you. May I have those teeth?"

"May I have your story? Just for my records." She picked up her notebook. "All vets keep records."

Yann shied away from the small lined book, his horse's hooves clattering backwards on the floor and his boy's fists clenching.

"You must not write any record of my visit! Written words are very powerful. What have you written in there?"

"Keep your voice down!"

He repeated, more quietly but just as urgently, "What have you written, healer's child?"

"Just your name, Yann, and your injury – cut to back right leg. Nothing else."

"Destroy the page."

"Why?"

"Tear it out and burn it. There could be such trouble if anyone knows."

"If anyone knows what?"

"That I have been here. Why I have been here."

"Okay. You want me to destroy this page, and you

want me to give you these teeth. And I want your story. Which I will not write down, I promise."

Yann shook his head. "It is not my story. It is a secret and it is not my secret. I have promised not to tell."

"You promised to grant my wish."

"Are you sure you don't want a puppy, or a kitten, or a sparkly dress, or a pumpkin coach to a handsome prince's palace?" Yann grinned, and so did Helen.

"No, I just want an answer to my question."

"That's all? An answer. So easy to ask for."

He scowled again, but not at her. Perhaps he was thinking.

"I cannot break my promise. But I can ask to be freed from it. If you will destroy that page now, before my eyes, I will come back tomorrow, to tell you what I can. And tomorrow you can give me the teeth."

So Helen ripped out the page, lit a match from her Mum's odds and ends drawer and burnt it to ash. Then she hauled on the big sliding door to let Yann out. He didn't move.

"Take the teeth out of your pocket, healer's child. It is not a safe place to keep them, so near to your skin."

She moved her hand to her pocket, then hesitated, wondering if it was a trick. Was he going to grab the teeth, and break his promise?

Yann snorted. "Wait until I have gone, if you don't trust me. But keep them hidden at least an arm's length from you or any other breathing creature. Not in a pocket, nor a bed, nor anywhere you keep food."

"Are the teeth poisonous? Have you been poisoned? Your leg isn't swollen."

"No, but they are the teeth of a creature controlled

by evil, and it is not wise to keep evil close. I will take them to a safe place tomorrow. Look for me when the sun goes down."

He was hardly limping as he left the surgery. He trotted across the garden, jumped smoothly over the fence and cantered into the darkness of the field and the hills beyond.

Helen didn't hear the rustling in the bushes as the creature hidden there wriggled, trying to decide whether to follow the boy or watch the girl.

She turned back into the surgery, and took the teeth out of her pocket. She put them on the work surface. Not too near her.

She cleared all the rubbish away, sprayed disinfectant and tidied the shelves so there were no gaps where she'd removed supplies. Then she dropped the teeth into an empty swab packet, folded the top over, and left the surgery.

She pulled the door gently behind her, and let herself quietly back into the house. She looked around the hall for a hiding place, and decided to slip the packet into the toe of a black welly that was too small for her and too big for her sister. Then she washed her hands thoroughly.

She said goodnight to her Dad in the study and to her Mum in the bath, and blew a kiss to her little sister in the nursery. Then she went to bed.

Just before she fell asleep, she realized that the boy had never even asked her name. And she didn't think he'd said "please" once either. If he didn't come back, she wouldn't mind one bit.

Chapter 2

Helen woke up before her alarm the next morning. She had a whole winter's day to get through before Yann came back to tell her his story.

She tiptoed downstairs before anyone else was awake, and rattled the welly in the hall. The packet of teeth was still there. Then she crept into the small animal surgery, where her Mum examined dogs and cats on a black rubber-topped table. The small room was crowded with leather chairs, a dark wooden desk, and glass-fronted shelves that held her Mum's university books.

Helen started running her finger along the shelves of veterinary reference books. She should have done this last night, before she stitched up that leg. She checked the index of the heaviest book, but couldn't find any mention of eleven-year-old girls stitching centaurs' legs.

So instead she looked through an old book called *First Aid for Ponies and Horses,* which had been her Mum's when she was a girl. Her fingers flicked past teeth, hooves and colic, until she reached the chapter on wounds. She found some drawings of a leg wound being treated. The stitches were much neater than her stitches had been, but the skin was held together in the same way. And her modern bandage and tape were much tidier and less bulky than that in the book.

The chapter ended with how to care for a wound as it healed: letting it air, changing dressings and keeping an eye out for swelling or infection. Helen grimaced at a faded photo of a pus-covered leg. She'd better check the wound tonight ... if Yann did keep his promise and come back.

Everyone else was getting up now, so she went back to her room, dressed in her school pinafore and blouse, and went downstairs for breakfast. She was halfway down the stairs when she heard a clip clop, clip clop coming from the kitchen and a little voice called out, "Horsie, look, horsie!"

Helen couldn't believe that Yann would return in daylight, and actually come into the house. But then she couldn't quite believe he'd appeared last night either.

She jumped down the last six steps, whirled herself round the bottom banister, and sprinted towards the sound of the hooves.

She spun on her toes, looking round the warm untidy kitchen. She saw the huge wooden table in the middle of the room, the piles of newspapers and empty jam jars in the corners, and the heaps of dishes and books on the blue and yellow units.

And she saw her little sister sitting in her high chair, banging two empty yoghurt pots together. *Clip clop, clip clop.* "Horsie, Hen, horsie!"

"What's the rush, speedy?" Dad asked Helen, as she sat down hard on her chair.

"I thought there was a horse in here!" She laughed a bit shakily.

"I *am* a horsie!" said Nicola.

"She is a horsie," agreed Dad. "We'll put on her reins and walk you to school if you hurry up with your breakfast."

Then Mum stamped in. "Who's been in my large animal surgery this morning? It's an absolute mess!"

Helen thought of her quick tidy up last night. She didn't think she'd left the surgery in a mess, but then Mum and Helen often disagreed about what a tidy bedroom looked like, so she supposed it could be her fault.

She couldn't possibly admit what she had been doing in there, so she was trying to think of a plausible story when Nicola yelled, "I'm a horsie, clip clop!"

"Oh Nicola. Were you being a horsie in the horse surgery?"

"Clip clop."

Helen's Mum assumed that was a "yes," so she turned to Dad and said, "Alasdair, you really must keep an eye on her when I'm in the shower. She's wrecked the place, and there are lots of dangerous blades and needles that she could cut herself on."

"Can I help you un-wreck the place?" Helen offered, hoping to find out what her Mum thought was tidy, so that she could cover her traces if she needed to use the surgery again tonight.

"Do you have time before you go to school?"

"Yes, if Nicola will canter all the way up the lane."

"Well, thank you. That would be a help."

Helen followed her Mum out of the house and towards the surgery. She stopped in surprise at the sliding door.

This was not anyone's idea of tidy.

All the drawers were open, with their plastic and metal contents dragged out. Boxes on the shelves had been knocked over, spilling gloves and thread everywhere. The yellow bags for clinical waste had been tipped out of the bins, so there were heaps of swabs and syringes and animal hair on the floor. And the filing cabinet had been emptied, so brown folders and white paper were scattered on top of everything else.

"It wasn't like this last night!" Helen blurted out.

"Last night?" her Mum asked, giving her a funny look.

"When I came to get you after Mr MacDonald called about his sheep. It wasn't like this then." Helen tried to sound convincing.

"No, I don't usually make this much mess when I'm working. How do you think Nicola got up to the top shelves?"

"Climbed on the drawers, maybe? She thought she was a monkey last week, so she got a lot of climbing practice."

Helen felt a bit guilty about letting her sister take the blame, when she suspected that this chaos wasn't the work of a toddler.

"You aren't annoyed with Nicola, are you?" she asked, sliding the folders back in the filing cabinet.

"No, she's only wee, and toddlers get into everything. It's my fault for leaving the door open, I've known for weeks it doesn't shut securely any more. You have to bang it about twenty times before it clicks and locks. I'll get it fixed as soon as I get a minute. Are you putting those in order?"

"MNOPQR ..." Helen muttered. "I hope so."

Wearing thick protective gloves, her Mum was putting waste to be incinerated into a yellow bag. She looked a bit puzzled at the large pile of bloody swabs, so Helen tried to distract her.

"Do Harry MacDonald and his sheep go before or after Hector McDonald and his organic goats? How do you separate the Macs, the Mcs and the Ms?" Her Mum sighed and came over to show her.

Helen trotted with her Dad and Nicola along the lane towards Clovenshaws Primary School. The Eildon hills appeared, as icy clouds of vapour above the River Tweed floated up in the mild winter sun, revealing the fields carved into the land by walls and fences.

She knew the Scottish Borders had been trampled and crushed by many armies in years gone by, but as she looked at the pale green land around her, she wondered what destructive forces had marched across the land last night, through their garden and into her mother's surgery.

Who had wrecked it? And why? Had they been looking for something Yann had left behind? Or the notes he had forced her to destroy? Or the teeth she had insisted on keeping?

She had some real questions for Yann now, rather than just curiosity and a wish for an interesting story. If he was bringing danger behind him, then perhaps she should just change his dressing tonight, and say, "Goodbye and don't come back."

Or maybe she should hear his story first.

She spent many quiet moments at school wondering what that story would be. What tale could involve high walls, sharp teeth, and boys with horses' legs? What could explain someone, or something, searching her Mum's surgery in the middle of the night?

At lunchtime, sitting on the benches near the infant playground, she and her best friend, Kirsty, were waving at Kirsty's littlest sister, who was a very small and very nervous Primary One. Kirsty was describing a TV programme about a gang of children outwitting an evil genius, but Helen was only half listening to her best friend's tale of chases and mysteries. She was hugging her knees to her chest, watching the little ones playing running games, and thinking about her own real life mystery.

"Are you going to watch it tonight, Helen?" Kirsty asked. "It's really good!"

"I might. Or I might have something more exciting to do."

"Nothing is more exciting than a good story!"

Helen smiled and agreed.

Helen stayed at school for an hour after the bell went, rehearsing yet again for the school's Christmas Eve concert in the gym hall. She played the fiddle with the rest of the school's small orchestra, but she was also going to perform a solo. As they rehearsed the Sugar Plum Fairy's dance for the last time, she watched the sky get a little darker and realized that the sun was setting. She had to get home.

Helen already had her violin in its case and was following Kirsty out of the door when the music teacher said, "Helen, can you stay for a couple of minutes, so we can work on your solo before it gets too dark?"

"I'm sorry, Mr Crombie, I can't. I have to go right now."

As the rest of the pupils clattered their instruments away, Mr Crombie spoke quietly so only Helen could hear. "I know doing a solo is a bit stressful, especially when I've invited the director of the summer school you want to go to next year to come and hear you play. This is your chance to impress her.

"But an audition isn't a magic trick, Helen. You don't have to pull a surprise out of a hat at the very last minute. You can play a piece we all know. It doesn't have to be original or unusual.

"Look, I can't help you perform at your best if I don't know what you're playing. Do you know yourself yet? Would you rather wait a year or so, and see what summer schools are available when you are older? I could cancel the director."

"No!" Helen tried to sound calm and confident. "Please don't do that. I am ready to do this now. I'll have the perfect piece of music ready in plenty of time."

Mr Crombie smiled. "I'm delighted to hear that. And if you do have a piece selected and rehearsed, then I look forward to hearing it at the next rehearsal."

Helen dashed out of school and across the playground, not sure if she was more annoyed with Mr Crombie for doubting that she could find and learn a simple piece of music in a couple of days, or with herself for not having done it yet. There were plenty of tunes she could play, she just wanted to play one that was absolutely perfect for her and her violin. But what if that perfect piece of music didn't exist?

She jogged along the narrow road in the growing dark, going as fast as she could with a violin case, a school bag and a lunch box.

When Yann had said "look for me when the sun goes down," had he meant this early? Just when the sun was setting? Or much later, when it was pitch black? And where would he be? In the garden? In the lane? Surely not in the surgery?

She sprinted through the gate, and searched the greying garden. It was empty, except for rustling bushes and shifting branches. She went in the back door, dumped her bags in the middle of the kitchen floor and shouted, "Hello, I'm home!"

There was no answer. The house was very quiet.

She went into the hall. The computer room light was on, and the door was closed. So Dad was working. The living room light was on, and the door was open. She heard her Mum reading a book about baby animals to Nicola.

"I'm home!" she yelled. She ran upstairs, changed out of her school clothes and rushed back into the garden for another look.

A huge two-headed shape leapt over the back fence straight at her.

Chapter 3

The huge shape landed gently on the grass, and stopped just in front of Helen.

It was Yann, with a girl on his back, and a bird flying round their heads.

"Greetings, healer's child."

"Good evening, Yann."

"I've come for the teeth that bit me, and to pay your price."

Suddenly light bounced into the garden as the kitchen window lit up. Someone was making tea.

Yann stepped sideways out of the brightness. Helen ducked down, and whispered, "We can't talk out here."

Yann turned towards the surgery doors.

"No, that's too near the house. Let's go into the garage."

The garage was an old barn, in the furthest corner of the garden. Even with the family's car and her Mum's Landrover by the doors, a pile of rusty tools in a corner, and some damp old furniture along the back wall, there was still plenty of space for them all.

Helen switched on the light and the small heater she was allowed to use in the winter, so she could practise music out here without disturbing the whole family. Then she looked at her guests.

Yann was looking sulky, but he didn't look in pain.

The girl who slid off his back and stood leaning against his neck had long, sleek, dark hair and big dark eyes, with almost no white showing. She looked slim and fit, but her cheeks and bare arms were plump and smooth. On this cold winter's evening she was wearing only a sleeveless grey dress, made of a shining swirling material.

Helen looked up at the bird they had brought with them, flying among the dusty wooden rafters.

But she wasn't a bird at all. She had wings, she had feathers and she was fluttering and swooping. But she also had blonde bunches, a purple dress, and arms, legs and head just like a doll.

If Nicola saw her she would shout "Fairy!" and giggle in delight.

But Helen didn't believe in fairies. Helen was far too old for that. Yann might think he could surprise her or make her ask daft questions, but she was determined not to look foolish in front of his friends.

She just said, as calmly as she could manage, "Aren't you going to introduce us, Yann?"

Yann turned to the girl beside him, and waved his arm at Helen.

"This is ... ah ..."

Then Yann frowned, as he realized he hadn't asked her name last night.

Helen grinned. "I'm Helen Strang."

The girl beside Yann smiled. "I'm Rona."

The maybe-fairy flew to a few inches in front of Helen's nose. "I'm Lavender. Pleased to meet you." Her voice was as high and small as Helen's little sister's, but it wasn't at all childish, it was quick and clever. Her tiny face was brightened by a sweet smile, but her pale blue eyes were steady and wise.

Now Helen wished she'd said, "I'm Helen, I'm a school girl, or a fiddler or a human girl." Then these fanciful people might have told her what they were, as well as their names, because even the girl, who had no wings and the same number of arms and legs as Helen, did not look entirely human.

Would it be rude to ask? There was a long silence. Well, then, she'd be the healer's child again.

"How's your leg, Yann?"

"It's healing."

"Can I have a look?"

She took a step forward, but Yann took a step back.

"I should change the dressing, and check for infection."

"My leg is fine. I came for the teeth, and to tell you your story. But I had to ask the others if I could tell you. Rona and Lavender offered to come with me, so they could ..."

Lavender broke in. "So we could meet you. We were curious. We don't get to see humans much, because we don't want them to see us. I wanted to see you and your house and your clothes and your ..."

Rona said, "I didn't come out of curiosity. I see enough people when I'm a seal. I needed to know that you would not break our trust before I would let Yann break his promise to us."

Her voice was very beautiful. Not piercing like Lavender's nor dismissive like Yann's, but slow, rhythmic and gentle like rolling water.

Helen couldn't help asking, "When are you a seal?"

"Most of the time. But when I want to be with my friends on land, then I shed my seal skin and walk."

"Are you a mermaid?"

Rona smiled, showing tiny sharp white teeth, nearer in size to Nicola's baby teeth than Helen's big ones.

"A mermaid? No. They don't like cold northern waters. They stay in sunny places where the sea is like a mirror and they can watch their reflection all day. I am a selkie. I am one of the seal people and I sing the songs of the sea."

She spoke the last words proudly as if it was a hard skill to learn.

"Do you always have wings, or do you change too?" Helen asked the girl flying above her head.

Lavender turned a full circle in the air. "I'm always the same, more's the pity. Always small, always in purple, always overlooked."

Yann smirked at Helen. He knew this wasn't the answer she had wanted.

He let the silence stretch just a little more.

Then he spoke. "Lavender is a fairy. Not the tooth fairy but a real fairy nonetheless. And she is one of those who hold this secret. I can tell you our story, but only if you take a pledge that you will keep it secret. That you will not write it down, nor tell it to anyone ... any human person, fabled beast or true animal. That you will hold the secret in your heart and never let it go."

"No," said Helen.

"No?"

"No. I can't promise to keep a secret I haven't heard yet. You might have done something terrible. You might be planning to do something terrible. You might be bringing danger on yourselves and others. You have already brought trouble to my family; my mother's surgery was broken into and wrecked last night. So I will not promise to keep a secret if you tell me something I should tell my parents or the police. The easiest way to keep promises is not to make ones you might break."

Helen folded her arms and stared at Yann.

Yann folded his arms and stared back.

"Fine! Keep the teeth. Keep your dressings. We'll leave you to your safety and contentment and boredom. Come, friends, time to go."

"No," said Rona. "I trust her. Tell her."

"You trust her? She's just said she won't promise."

"That's why I trust her. If she had promised without thinking, just out of curiosity, she wouldn't really mean it. But she didn't promise, because she will think hard about the consequences of what we tell her. Yann, if we had thought that hard on Sunday, we wouldn't be in trouble now. Tell her, and she might be able to help."

Yann looked at Lavender.

"Do you agree? Do you trust her?"

Lavender flew onto his shoulder. "Oh, yes, let's tell her our story. In the olden times, quests and adventures always fared better when we involved humans."

"Is it a long story?" asked Helen.

"Not days long, no," said Yann.

"Should we sit down?" She pointed at a saggy old couch against the back wall.

"You sit. I prefer to stand."

Helen sat at one end of the brown and orange couch. Rona stretched out elegantly at the other, smoothing down her soft grey dress. Lavender fluttered over to the arm beside Helen, and perched on it, dangling her tiny legs.

And Yann began.

"Many years ago, the fabled beasts shared the earth with humans, but then the humans learnt to farm and your numbers grew, and you needed more and more land. Then you learnt to harness the energy in the earth and the lightning, and your numbers grew even more and your cities spread everywhere.

"And now there are so many humans, the fabled beasts that are left must hide in secret places in the folds and on the edges of maps. Our numbers have fallen, so that in some generations, in some places, our peoples may have only one or two young.

"Perhaps when there were many of us, centaurs kept to themselves on the grassy slopes, selkies stayed on the rocky coasts and fairies stayed close to their flowers.

"But it's hard to grow up alone, and the children of the fabled beasts have to make friends with each other, or else we have no friends at all.

"So the three of us, and some other fabled beasts, meet when we can in quiet places, and we talk."

Rona explained, "We talk about our parents and their rules, and our teachers and their rules, and we talk about how we can change the world."

Lavender added, "And we share moans and groans, and we do each other's hair and feathers and fur and scales, and plan parties and play silly jokes and it's a lot more fun than watching your aunties do finding spells all day."

Yann sighed. "But lately we have grown bored. And two days ago we did a foolish thing."

"Not 'we' Yann," Lavender said sharply, "We didn't *all* think it was a good idea. It was your idea. *You* did a foolish thing."

"We were all there when it was done," said Rona calmly, "We must all bear some responsibility."

Yann spoke in a voice so quiet it was almost a whisper. "A foolish thing was done, and we have all pledged to put it right."

He raised his voice again, and looked at Helen, "We stole a precious object. We called it borrowing. We thought we had a right to it. But we have scared it and lost it, and we may have driven it into the arms of the one we fear the most."

"What do you fear the most?" asked Helen.

"No. I will not start with the worst. I will start with the best."

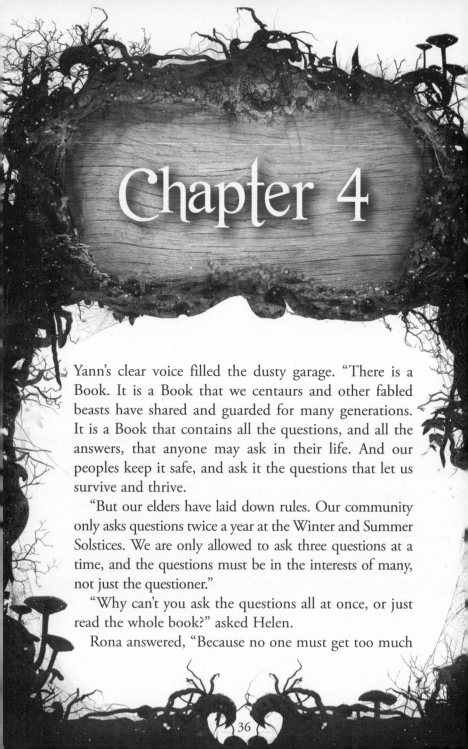

Chapter 4

Yann's clear voice filled the dusty garage. "There is a Book. It is a Book that we centaurs and other fabled beasts have shared and guarded for many generations. It is a Book that contains all the questions, and all the answers, that anyone may ask in their life. And our peoples keep it safe, and ask it the questions that let us survive and thrive.

"But our elders have laid down rules. Our community only asks questions twice a year at the Winter and Summer Solstices. We are only allowed to ask three questions at a time, and the questions must be in the interests of many, not just the questioner."

"Why can't you ask the questions all at once, or just read the whole book?" asked Helen.

Rona answered, "Because no one must get too much

unearned or unlearned knowledge. Wisdom is found not only in the answers but also in the journey to find them. To know all your life's answers too soon would give you too much power and not enough curiosity."

Yann sighed. "But we were impatient. We have so much to learn, about how to live in a world that is hardly ours any more. We wondered if our parents were making the right decisions for us, and we wondered if the Book could give us guidance.

"So we called on our skills and magic to draw the Book from its place of safety. Then we opened it. But before we could ask it anything important, it took fright and flew off.

"We don't know if it was angered by our impertinent questions, or if it sensed the presence of darker creatures who wanted it too. But now the Book is gone, and we must find it.

"We must find it before our parents realize it is gone. Before my father says the words to release the Book from its place of safety for the Winter Solstice Gathering at the end of the week."

Rona took a deep breath. "If we tell our parents, they would help ..."

Yann interrupted, "We have discussed this. We must be responsible and sort it out ourselves."

"We should be responsible enough to admit our mistake and ask for help."

"It wasn't just a mistake, Rona, it was a crime and we would be punished for it. If we can find the Book before the ceremony, they may never know it was gone."

Lavender's little voice broke into the argument. "We might even be banned from seeing each other if they find out. I couldn't bear that, could you?" She flew to Rona and hugged her.

Yann trotted in a tight circle round the garage, then returned to his place in front of the couch. "But our parents' anger is not the worst of it. We must retrieve the Book and take it back to a place of safety before the Master of the Maze finds it, or it could mean the end of our world."

Helen asked, as she was clearly meant to, "The Master of the Maze?"

"The Master of the Maze was cast out from the community of fabled beasts many years ago because he wanted to read the whole Book, and use its power to make our numbers grow as fast as those of humans. Our elders say he would use the Book to overturn the balance between questions and answers, wonder and truth, wisdom and facts.

"He has waited for generations to get his hands on the Book, and now we may have given it to him. And he will use its answers to gain power for himself."

"What is he? What kind of creature?" Helen asked.

"He is the Master of the Maze. The creature at the heart of the puzzle. The Minotaur."

"A Minotaur? Like you? Half man, half animal?"

Yann reared up. His front legs churned in the air, and his head reached up to the rafters. Helen forced herself back into the couch's saggy cushions, away from the slashing hooves.

Yann crashed back down, shouting, "I am not like him! I am not an animal! I am a noble centaur. We have been leading the fabled beasts safely and honourably for more years than there are stories."

Rona put her hand on Helen's arm. It felt a little damp. "Helen, it's not the animal part that's the problem. The Master is mostly man. More than the rest of us. A man's body, with a man's heart and a man's greed, but the head of a black bull. He is very strong, and he is the leader of those who crave chaos and bloodshed."

"Well, they certainly left chaos in my Mum's surgery."

"We are sorry that we have led danger to your door." Rona stroked Helen's arm, then took her hand away.

Yann humphed. "So, that is the story. That is all I owe you. It is our secret and our problem, and need be no more concern of yours."

Helen thought for a moment, then said slowly, "But if the Master wants answers so he can increase your population to challenge human numbers, then it is my problem and my family's problem."

Yann shrugged. "But you humans are not taking very good care of the earth, are you? Would it be any worse if fabled beasts were in charge? If he were to ask the Book how to increase our numbers and reduce yours, then we could get back to equilibrium. More centaurs and selkies and fewer humans might make a greener land and a bluer sea."

"Yann!" Rona said indignantly, "The Master doesn't want more centaurs and selkies and fairies and phoenixes, he wants more of his own kind. He wants more minotaurs and basilisks and manticores. And he doesn't want equilibrium, he wants empire. Worst of all, he wants to know all the answers at once, and that is simply not allowed."

Helen looked back at Yann, who was glowering at the ground.

"So how will you find the Book?" she asked.

He didn't look at Helen but he did answer her question.

"The Book left us a clue. We hope it wants to be found, but to find it we must answer its questions, as it has so often answered ours. We hope the Master doesn't answer the questions first, or his minions will be ahead of us on the trail, not behind."

"And was it one of the Master's creatures that bit you?"

"I think so, yes. As I leapt over the wall of the garden, something bit me and when I kicked my leg free, my skin ripped. But I didn't see what kind of animal it was. If I could see the teeth, I might be able to work it out."

"I'll go and get the teeth for you." Helen wanted a moment to think by herself.

She opened the door, and was hit in the face by a flurry of feathers and claws. She slammed the door shut, but a heavy bird was already tangled in her hair.

As she tried frantically to haul the bird off, she could feel its clawed feet scraping her scalp and hard feathers poking towards her eyes. Her fingers, reaching high above her, couldn't get a grip on the flapping wings. She had her teeth gritted against the scream of panic that was growing in her chest.

Rona was suddenly beside her, saying calmly, "He's a friend, Helen, he's a friend, stay still."

Helen lowered her hands, and stood still, her legs shaking and her shoulders crawling up to her ears. Rona and Lavender untangled the bird, and while Rona smoothed the bird's feathers, Lavender sat on Helen's shoulder and tidied her hair. Though Helen hadn't made a noise, her eyes were watering.

Yann walked quietly up and gave her a cloth from the workbench behind the car. "Wipe the sweat off your forehead," he said, without looking at her face. She took the slightly dusty cloth, and muttered, "Thanks." She wiped her face. Now she could look at the bird.

He was much bigger than Lavender. The size of a large cockerel, or even a goose. His slightly ruffled feathers were copper, orange and gold, and as he took off from Rona's hands, his long tail feathers flickered like flames. He could have been an exotic bird of paradise, or a very elegant cousin of the pheasants in the fields out the back.

Yann wasn't playing bad-tempered games now. He introduced the bird immediately. "This is Catesby. He's a phoenix. Catesby, this is the healer's child. Do you have news?"

Catesby clearly did have news, but as he squawked and swooped round the garage, Helen didn't have the faintest idea what it was. Yann and Rona were shocked into silence though and Lavender burst into tears.

Then Catesby was quiet and Yann announced, "We must leave now. One of our friends is hurt and has been followed home by the Master's creatures. We must go to her."

Helen asked, "Can I help?"

"What?"

"If one of your friends is hurt, can I help?"

"How? You told me last night you have none of your mother's healing skills and no interest in learning them."

Lavender flew into Yann's face. "How's your leg, Yann?"

Yann swatted her away.

Helen grinned. "All I need to help your friend tonight – like I helped you last night – is a first aid kit."

"What's a first aid kit?"

"The equipment most likely to be used out in the field. Swabs, dressings, basic medicines, needles and sutures. It can keep someone alive until the real healers get there. I can get a kit in a moment. What kind of ... friend is hurt?"

Yann just laughed. "You will not be able to stitch this one up. Your sharp little needles will be no good on Sapphire if she is cut."

"Why not?"

"Because even young dragons have scales as tough as slate. And how would you get to her? Can you gallop, human? Can you fly?"

Rona said, "She can ride on your back, Yann, just like I do. Aren't you strong enough for two?"

"I will not be ridden by a human. I will not be saddled and bridled and tamed!"

"I can go pretty fast on my bike," said Helen confidently.

"Over fields? And rivers? We have no more time to debate. We leave now."

"Wait! I'll get you the teeth, I'll just be a minute."

Helen rushed out of the garage, back into the house, and grabbed the swab packet from the welly. Then she went into her Mum's small animal surgery, and pulled out an exotic animals textbook that she and Nicola often borrowed for its pictures of zoo animals. She turned to the hooks on the back of the door, and grabbed the spare first aid kit, a green waterproof rucksack with a full set of supplies in it.

As she left the surgery she heard her Mum's voice from the living room. "Helen? Is that you? It's nearly teatime."

"Hi, Mum. I'm not hungry and I've got lots to do, so I'll see you at supper." She stomped noisily up to her room, then tiptoed back down again, hoping that her parents would think she was staying in her room all evening.

She pushed open the back door and slipped out into the garden. Yann and Rona were having a whispered argument just outside the garage door.

"Humans have enslaved my cousins for thousands of years. I will not become a farm animal just to take this human child out for a jaunt."

"You let *me* ride you."

"You are not human. You are a fellow fabled beast. You are a friend."

"She could be a friend too if you weren't so rude to her all the time," Rona said reasonably.

"She is human. They are not our friends. They are our problem."

"This human has offered to help. You cannot refuse help for Sapphire tonight that you sought for yourself last night."

Helen walked noisily up to them, hoping they would stop talking about her. She would like to help them, and be part of their adventure, but not if Yann disliked her this much.

She handed the kit and the book to Rona.

"Here. See if you can help your friend with this. I don't want to slow you down, and I really don't want to ride on him."

All the fabled beasts stared at the book.

Helen said, "It doesn't have a chapter on dragons, obviously, but there are some case studies on lizards and snakes that might be useful."

Then she handed the packet with teeth in it to Yann. "The teeth of the creature that bit you. I promised you could have them when you answered my question. If you get hurt again, any of you, I will help if I can. Good luck."

She stepped away. Yann snorted through his nose, and hacked at the grass with a front hoof. Then he stood right in front of Helen and demanded, "Do you ride? Do you have a pampered pony somewhere? Do you take her to pony club gymkhanas and jump her over little striped poles?"

"No. I prefer my bike. You don't have to groom it, feed it or muck out. And you don't have to be polite to it either."

"But can you ride? Would you fall off?"

Helen said carefully, "I won't fall off, if you don't throw me off."

"I will only throw you off, human girl, if you try to tell me where to go."

"I don't know where your dragon is, so I can't tell you where to go."

"Climb up, then. Put your arms round my waist, and use your legs and back to keep your balance. Don't dig your feet into my sides, and don't tell me what to do."

So Helen hauled herself up on Yann's back, and Rona climbed on more elegantly behind her. Lavender sat on Helen's shoulder, grasping her hair, and Rona put the green rucksack on her own back. With Catesby soaring above them, Yann leapt the back fence and was out of the garden and into the fields beyond.

Helen took a deep breath and held on tight.

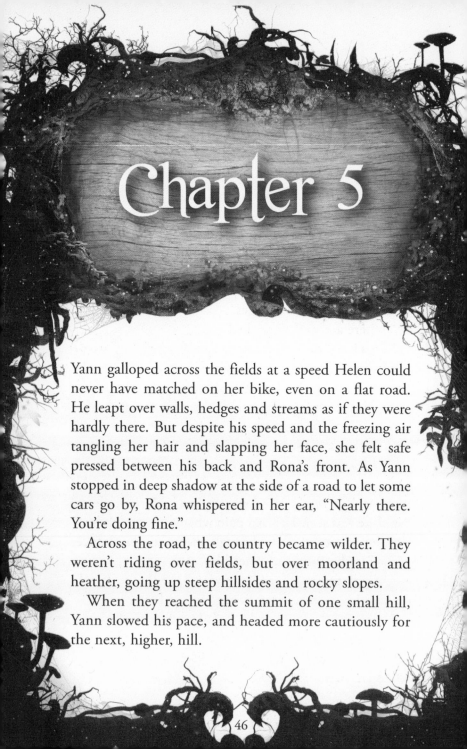

Chapter 5

Yann galloped across the fields at a speed Helen could never have matched on her bike, even on a flat road. He leapt over walls, hedges and streams as if they were hardly there. But despite his speed and the freezing air tangling her hair and slapping her face, she felt safe pressed between his back and Rona's front. As Yann stopped in deep shadow at the side of a road to let some cars go by, Rona whispered in her ear, "Nearly there. You're doing fine."

Across the road, the country became wilder. They weren't riding over fields, but over moorland and heather, going up steep hillsides and rocky slopes.

When they reached the summit of one small hill, Yann slowed his pace, and headed more cautiously for the next, higher, hill.

As he walked, Helen heard Rona whisper again, "We must be quiet now. We may not be alone."

Then Yann walked straight into a cliff.

Helen flinched, but the cliff opened suddenly into a narrow chasm, then a wider cave.

"You can get down now," said Yann.

Rona slid down, and so did Helen, her legs a bit wobbly and her arms stiff. Rona gave her the rucksack.

Yann turned to Helen. "You didn't dig your feet in. Thank you. Perhaps I won't make you walk home." It was very dark in the cave, and Helen couldn't tell if he was smiling and making a joke, or if he was serious. Perhaps he never made jokes.

"Where are we?" she asked.

"This is the back entrance to Sapphire's cave. Catesby thinks that something may have followed her after she was attacked, so we can't go straight in the front door. There is another way to her chamber through that tunnel there." He pointed to a black jagged oval at the back of the cave. "But it's too narrow and low for me, so I will leave you here and go round the front. If the front entrance is being watched I will lure or scare away the watcher. If it isn't, I will join you inside. Hurry, please. Sapphire was scared and in pain when Catesby left her."

Yann squeezed back through the narrow entrance, with Catesby fluttering after him.

"All girls together," said Lavender. "That's nice. If only we had time to talk about how annoying boys can be."

Helen was looking doubtfully at the blackness round her. "Do we have any light?"

"You have no light in that magic bag of yours?" asked Lavender.

"I didn't realize we were going under a hill, or I'd have brought a torch."

"Never mind. Even fledgling fairies can do light spells." Lavender produced a tiny stick from her dress and blew on it. The end blossomed into a ball of gentle light, not bright enough to make you squint when you looked directly at it, but bright enough for Helen to see the walls of the small cave. Now she could see dark scuttlings and shiftings on the rock around her.

She jumped. "What was that? Are there living things in here?"

"There are living things everywhere," said Rona. "These ones don't like light. They won't bother us. Let's go."

"Do you know the way? Have you used this back door before?"

"No," answered Lavender. "But Catesby says that Sapphire says that a knight looking for treasure got in this way when her grandfather was young. So I'm sure it will be fine."

Helen looked at Lavender. It was now bright enough to see her face. She was smiling. Did that mean she was joking, or that she was laughing at Helen's fears?

Helen said cautiously, "I suppose if the tunnel's blocked by a rockfall or something we can just turn round and come back out."

Lavender smiled even more charmingly. "Absolutely. So long as the rockfall is in front of us."

They entered the narrow tunnel. Lavender first with the light, then Helen, carrying the rucksack, then Rona.

Helen knew that most caves were formed by water dissolving holes in limestone. Every time she heard or felt a drip, she was sure that the water was dissolving the whole hill around her. The rocky ceiling looked as if it could crash down on her head any moment.

The threatening rock was a dull pencil-grey colour, but sometimes Lavender's light lit up a seam of a brighter mineral, slashing across the floor, walls or ceiling, looking like the rock had been torn apart and glued back together. Helen ran her finger along the tunnel wall. It seemed solid enough.

The tunnel had started too narrow and low to let a centaur through, and it kept getting smaller. The ceiling sloped down, the floor rose up and the walls came inwards. Soon Helen was walking with her head and shoulders stooped, her knees bent and her elbows pulled into her ribs to stop them banging on the bumpy walls. Adventures were more awkward than she had expected.

Lavender was dancing and swirling ahead of her, but then she could fit through a letterbox without ruffling her dress. Behind Helen, Rona was grunting with effort.

The tunnel wasn't level either. Sometimes the ache in Helen's thighs told her they were climbing uphill, and sometimes the ache in her knees told her they were walking downhill.

After a particularly long downhill trudge, Helen's feet began to splash through little puddles. As they went lower the puddles became a stretch of water. The water reached higher, over the top of her ankle boots, then up to her shins. It was so cold that she was surprised the surface wasn't crackling with ice.

"Can either of you swim?" Rona panted from behind her.

"No," replied Lavender.

"Yes," said Helen, "but I've never swum in a cave, nor in water this cold."

"My light would go out underwater anyway," said Lavender, "and if there isn't enough air between the water and the rock for me to fly, there won't be enough air for you two to breathe."

"Was the knight's armour rusty when he reached the dragon's chamber?" asked Helen.

"The story doesn't say, but that was hundreds of years ago, and caves can change quite quickly. Should we turn back?" Lavender looked at the two bigger girls behind her.

"We must be nearer the front door than the back now," said Helen, "and we don't want to turn round and go all that way again unless we have to. Perhaps you could fly on for a few moments, Lavender, and see if the tunnel goes lower into the water, or if it slopes back up to dry stone?"

Lavender didn't answer for a moment. Then she sniffed a little. "I suppose I have to. Don't go away."

She took a deep breath, and flew on ahead. Helen and Rona saw her light reflecting off the wet walls and water for a few moments, then the fairy turned a corner and they stood together in the bitter cold dark.

There was a gentle splashing as Rona moved nearer Helen, and the two girls held hands.

"Are you scared?" Rona whispered.

"Yes, are you?"

"Yes."

"Lavender must be more afraid. She's on her own," Helen pointed out.

"She has the light. We should have asked her to leave us some."

There was a long pause, during which they could hear

only drips and their own breathing. Helen imagined the drips slowly filling the pool until it reached their necks, mouths and noses. She was almost too numb to move even if the water rose over their heads.

"Why did you come with us?" Rona asked.

"I thought I could help. And Yann hasn't really finished his story. What wall did he leap over, and how was your dragon friend injured, and what clue has the Book left behind? I want to know how the story ends. Also, I don't think Yann likes me, and I wanted to show him that ... Och, I'm not sure ... that not all humans are bad. Not all people pamper ponies."

"Don't mind Yann. Everyone gets scared in different ways. Lavender gets all fluttery and bursts into tears, then takes tight hold of her wand and gets on with it. Catesby, as you saw, gets a bit clumsy. Yann gets very rude and touchy. But he feels responsible for all of us. If we fail to get the Book back, he will take all the blame on himself, even though he knows his father would never forgive him for shaming their tribe. And you fixed his leg, so he feels in your debt, which is always awkward. Also, you're a human child, and he's been taught that humans are dangerous and to be avoided at all costs. It's surprising he's talking to you at all really."

"So if I wasn't human, and I hadn't fixed his leg, and he wasn't scared and guilty, he would say please a bit more often, and maybe even tell jokes and do some juggling?"

Rona laughed. "Well no. Centaurs are always a bit stiff and proper. But he wouldn't be quite so rude if he wasn't quite so worried. And he definitely wouldn't have let you ride on his back if he didn't like you just a little bit."

"So, if Yann is rude, and Lavender cries, and Catesby gets tangled in people's hair, how do *you* deal with being scared?"

"I'm trying very hard to be calm right now," Rona said softly, "but when I get home I will need to do a lot of very loud singing."

"Singing?"

"Yes. Among my people I am learning to be a singer. And when I am happy or sad, or scared or worried, I sing about it until it becomes part of me and part of the sea and part of my people. Then it isn't so overwhelming."

"What songs do you sing?" Helen asked.

"Old songs about when fish were made of silver and gold. Ballads about humans and seals falling in love. Battle songs about killer whales and sharks. But I write my own too. I might write the story of our quest for the Book. If we ever find it."

The warmth and enthusiasm in Rona's voice made the cold water round Helen's feet easier to bear. "Would you sing the quest song to me, when you've finished it?"

"Yann said that you want to be a music-maker, not a healer like your mother. Do you sing?"

"A little, but mostly I play the violin. I like old tunes too, and I've written a few short pieces of my own as well. Right now I'm searching for a perfect piece of music; not perfect for everyone, just the absolutely right one to show how my violin and I play best together. It's ... it's hard to explain."

"You shouldn't try to explain music. Just play it. I know ... when we find the Book, I could sing the story and you could play it," Rona suggested, "Just for our friends, even if we can never tell anyone else."

"For our friends? That would be great. But will we find the Book?"

"I think so. I think with your help we will. Lavender was right. In the old stories, it has always been when the fabled beasts worked with humans that we defeated evil. And many of our best adventures have happened in the company of a human bard, musician or storyteller. You may be our bard. When we have healed Sapphire, and she has given us the clue, we will see if you can help us with that too."

Helen, who had never been any good at crosswords or quizzes, made a sceptical face in the darkness, but for this girl who talked so easily of 'our friends,' she would certainly try.

She squeezed Rona's hand, and they waited in the creeping black cold.

Then the black slowly lightened. At first the dark shadows got darker, then the wet areas shone, then Lavender and her light came round the corner.

"Hello! Are you there?" her little voice called.

"Here we are!"

"Oh, thank goodness. I thought I would never get back to you."

Lavender hugged Rona's neck, then flew to Helen and kissed her cheek.

"I'm not going ahead on my own ever again. Next time one of you can take some light and go and look."

"What did you see?" asked Helen.

"Well, the tunnel keeps going down for a short way, but then it definitely comes back up again, and the floor rises out of the water. But I can't tell how deep it gets first. Do you want to risk it?"

"Yes!" said both girls at once. Now they had light, and they were all together again, it seemed that they could do anything.

So they set off along the tunnel.

The water rose quickly now. Before they were round the corner, it was above their knees, then nearly to Helen's waist. It was very hard to push through its swirling cold heaviness.

"It goes uphill again soon, I promise," insisted Lavender. She repeated this promise several times, as the water got higher and higher.

"Do you want to turn back?" asked Rona.

Helen, concentrating on each slow step so she didn't slip into the deep water, just shook her head.

Finally the water started to get shallower. It was down to Helen's knees, her ankles, then just her toes again.

After that, the dry tunnel, however narrow, seemed like a footpath on an easy walk.

The girls strode along, whispering and laughing quietly. Wondering if they would get to the chamber before Yann and Catesby, wondering if Sapphire would have any food they could eat, hoping that she could light a small fire to dry them.

But then the tunnel came to an abrupt end. Suddenly, the only way forward was a tiny opening in a blank wall of rock.

"I'm not going through myself," Lavender sniffed, "Not on my own, not again."

Before Lavender could start to cry properly, Helen said, "Give me the light. If I can fit through, so can Rona."

"And if you can't? If you can't turn round, you might be stuck."

"You can just pull me back out again."

Helen took the rucksack off and handed it to Rona. "If I get through, just shove this after me."

Then she took the tiny glowing wand from Lavender and held it delicately in her right hand. It felt very fragile.

"No." She gave it back. "You two keep the light. I'll need both hands. I'll just feel my way through."

But Lavender said, "I can give you some light you don't need to hold." The fairy flicked her wand, and the light ball flew off. It streaked through the air, bounced off the wall of the cave, and came to a halt, hovering just in front of Helen. She blew at it, and the bright white ball bobbed away from her, then slowly returned.

Helen grinned. "Thank you." She crouched down by the gap, and heard a faint noise. A groaning or croaking.

"Is that your dragon friend?"

Rona crouched beside her, listened, then nodded. "We must be near her chamber now."

Helen put her arms, head and shoulders into the gap, and tried to push the rest of her body up and in. At first she thought she was stuck, and wondered how much it would hurt to be dragged back across all this rough rock. But with a few wriggles she got inside and then pushed herself further on with her toes.

In the light of the little ball ahead of her, she saw cracks into which she could fit her fingers to drag herself forward. Then the space widened a little and she could get up from her tummy and use her knees and elbows too. She edged round a slight bend, and saw a grey circle ahead. The way out! The air seemed slightly warmer too.

She called behind her, "I think I'm nearly there. Give me a couple of minutes, then follow me."

She forced herself towards the exit, and the grey circle widened to reveal that the tunnel opened out just above the floor of a cave, which was dimly lit by a hole high in the ceiling.

At the other side of the cave, on a raised platform of rock, a lizard crouched on a nest of wire and bricks and pebbles.

As Helen got an idea of the size of the cave from some bats fluttering in at the hole in the roof, she realized that the cave was bigger than her school gym hall; the nest was made from metal swords, gold crowns and jewels; and the lizard was the size of a small van.

This was the dragon. And the dragon was crying. Not delicate little sobs like Lavender, but great roaring howls.

The dragon was bright blue, with long silver claws, and a vast tail coiled round its whole length. Its eyes were closed, but its jaws, resting on its front legs, were open. It was breathing out ragged clouds of smoke as it wept. It had long curved white teeth and a forked tongue which vibrated with every gasping cry.

Helen couldn't see any sign of Yann or Catesby. But she had to get out of the hole, so that Rona and Lavender could fit through.

There was no elegant or quick way out of the narrow tunnel, because she couldn't get her feet out until she had lowered the rest of her body down to the ground. She tried to be quiet, but as she bumped onto the rocky floor of the cave, she dislodged some stones. That set off a flurry of bats from the ceiling, and the dragon lifted its head and roared.

Helen yelled, "I'm a friend of Yann's!" as the

dragon clattered off its metal pile and stumbled in her direction. It didn't look very seriously injured; all four legs were working and so was its fire-breathing equipment.

It blasted jets of flame through the air towards the flying bats and the rolling pebbles, towards anything moving and making a noise. Helen scrambled behind a pile of rusty metal and hid there, hoping the dragon couldn't see her.

She smelt smoke and heard the scrape of claws getting nearer. All of a sudden, Helen wished she hadn't tried quite so hard to persuade her strange new friends to take her with them tonight.

Chapter 6

"Frass! Frass!"

"Master, I am here."

"Where are the young idiots now?"

"They have left the human house, and gone to the dragon's lair. But the dragon is badly injured. They won't be going anywhere else tonight. I have a family of weasels stationed at the cave entrance, and another at the human dwelling, so we can keep track of them all."

"And you drove the dragonling off before she found the clue?"

"Oh no, she had the clue with her when she fled."

"What! Why did you allow that to happen, you flea-bitten goat-legged failure?"

"We already know what the clue says, Master, and I thought that if the children of the fabled beasts had it too, then if they managed to work it out before we do, we could simply follow them to the Book."

"You thought that a gang of half-grown half-witted half-beasts would work it out before *me?* I am the Master of the Maze, the Lord of the Labyrinth, the prince at the heart of the puzzle. Do you doubt that I can best them at a simple riddle?"

"No of course not, Master, of course not. But the clue is meant for them, sir, not us, and the Book may have designed it so that only they can work it out."

"I see. And the human girl? Does she know anything valuable? Will they be going back to her abode? Is it worth keeping watch?"

"The weasels report that the fabled beasts have taken the girl with them to the cave. She is still helping them. Perhaps she now knows their secret?"

"A human child? Working with the centaurs and fairies and other fluffy beasts? That is not auspicious. Watch her. Watch her family. Find out who her friends are, and what is precious to her. But do not be seen. Use native creatures where you can. And bring me the copy of the clue again. Then give me peace and quiet to think."

Helen crouched behind the rusty metal as the dragon scraped and grunted towards her. She had an ointment for burns in her first aid kit, but she didn't think it would be enough to save her if this dragon hit her directly with a flame. Should she call out again and say she was a friend? But if the dragon couldn't understand her, or was in too much pain to listen, then a shout would just give her position away.

Then she heard a clatter of stones, and saw Rona roll out of the hole in the wall a few feet away, pushing the green rucksack out in front of her. There was another roar and another jet of misdirected flame.

Rona yelled, "Oh cool down, Sapphire! It's Rona and Lavender, and the healer's child. We've come to help."

Helen heard a crash and another grating sob. She peered cautiously round the pile of metal. The dragon had slumped on the floor of the cave just a couple of clawed footsteps away.

Lavender flew out of the hole and darted round the cave, leaving floating balls of light in a circle round their heads.

Now Helen could see that the dragon's eyes were purple, puffy and oozing pus. She also saw that the tangled pile of metal she'd hidden behind was a heap of rusty armour. Perhaps the knights of long ago had indeed waded through that pool.

Rona was standing by the dragon, stroking her head and singing gently. Helen stepped nearer, feeling safer now that her friends were here, but the dragon raised its blind head and roared. Helen stumbled back again.

Rona explained, "She doesn't like humans. She says that all humans ever want from dragons is their treasure. She won't let you near her trove."

Rona soothed the dragon with her hands and voice. "Sapphire, my friend, she is here to help. She healed Yann's leg and she can heal you too."

The dragon roared again and blew a small jet of smoke in Helen's direction.

Lavender flew down, having flicked lights all round the cave.

"Oi!" she snapped. "We came all the way here to help you, Sapphire, and I know you're scared and sore, but remember your manners, and let this healer's child have a look at you."

The dragon roared once more. Sparks danced across the floor.

"I have a gift for Sapphire," Helen said quietly. "I have some treasure to add to her trove." She took a glittering string of beads from round her neck. It was a necklace she had made with Kirsty one rainy weekend, made of plastic pearls and rainbow-coloured teardrops, but it sparkled in the magical light.

"It's beautiful," said Lavender firmly. "And it will fit nicely on your front leg."

It was threaded on strong elastic, so it did indeed stretch over the dragon's claws, to fit round her front left leg.

The dragon stopped roaring. She grunted and whistled creakily. Rona knelt by her head to listen.

Then the selkie turned to Helen. "Sapphire thanks you for the gift, but she cannot see it, as she has been blinded by the Master's creatures. Can you help her?"

"How was she blinded?" asked Helen, picking up her rucksack and trying to concentrate on the dragon's eyes, rather than her teeth and hot breath.

"She was collecting the Book's riddle from the walled garden, and someone knocked a tower of stones down onto her. Her scales protected her body, but chips of rock and slate got into her eyes. Catesby had to guide her home because her vision was blurred. Since he left, her eyes have got worse, and now she can't see at all. She is very frightened."

Helen opened the first aid kit, and pulled out the exotic animals book. She found lizards' eyes in the index, and studied that page before noticing pictures of snakes' eyes on the opposite page. She looked up at the dragon's eyes, and frowned. Sapphire's eyes looked more like snakes' eyes than lizards' eyes.

She then put the book down and spoke directly to the dragon.

"Do you shed your skin?"

Sapphire's throat rumbled and she nodded.

"Do you shed the scales over your eyes?"

Sapphire nodded again.

"Hmmmmm." Helen studied the snake pages again.

"Right," she muttered. "If you had eyelids and tear ducts I could just wash the bits of grit out, but instead you have see-through scales that cover your eyes, and the grit is trapped underneath. If I don't clear it out, it will stay there until the next time you shed your skin, and by then you might be blinded for ever."

The dragon groaned.

Helen hunted in her bag and got out an eyedropper the length of her littlest finger. She looked up at the dragon, whose eyes were the size of bicycle wheels. Helen sighed and put the eyedropper back. She dug out the biggest syringe in the bag. Then she broke the seal on a bottle of sterile saline, filled the syringe, and walked right up to the dragon. "Stay still," she said calmly.

Using a sterile swab to clear the pus and dust away, Helen could see gravel-sized bits of sharp, grey rock in the dragon's eyes. She gently eased the see-through scale away just enough to skoosh saline in and dislodge the stones.

She tried not to flinch at the gusts of hot breath on her legs, but at least they were drying her boots and jeans, and warming the rest of her up.

She finished the left eye, then moved round to the dragon's right one. She used the last of the salty liquid to shift the very last bit of grit, then found a length of bandage to dry the dragon's eyes.

She stepped back a little, and saw two huge, red-rimmed, silver eyes, now clear and shining, looking straight at her.

The dragon roared softly.

Rona explained, "Sapphire says thank you. She can see again, and she will forever be in your debt."

"My pleasure," said Helen, and she couldn't help grinning as she tidied all her equipment back into the bag.

"What's the book?" asked Lavender. "Is it your book?"

"No, it's my Mum's ..."

Helen was interrupted by a familiar clip clop clip clop, and she turned to see Yann trot into the cave through an opening in the far corner. Then Catesby swooped in, frightening more bats into a flurry of leathery wings.

Catesby fluttered anxiously round the dragon, peering at her eyes. Slightly out of breath, Yann asked, "Sapphire! Are you alright? Catesby said you were going blind!"

Sapphire grunted a couple of low notes and Lavender chirped, "She healed her! The human girl healed her ... with her book and her green bag!" But Yann didn't even look at Helen, he just kept questioning the blue dragon.

"Do you have the clue? Catesby says you managed to bring it with you."

Sapphire roared in triumph and flapped her wings, sending Lavender's balls of light crashing into each other.

Yann yelled, "Yes!" His boy hands punched the air, while his horse hooves pirouetted round the cave. "Let's see it, you fabulous fire breather!"

Rona said, "Wait. Let us do everything in its proper order. First tell us if there are watchers outside the cave."

"There were, but they were only weasels. Catesby picked a couple of them up in his talons and dropped them in a stream, then the rest were quite keen to leave. We waited until the wet weasels had slunk away and then we came in."

"So the Master is using weasels?" Lavender flew down to the long bandage on Yann's leg. "Might it have been a weasel that bit you, Yann?"

"A weasel?" He snorted. "Well, it was either a very big weasel, or a whole army of them."

Lavender laughed lightly. "So you say. Perhaps it was just one wee baby weasel. Poor you."

Helen said, "Whatever bit Yann, whether it was a weasel or a wolf, it was a vicious bite and it's a bad wound. I will need to look at it again tonight."

Rona tapped her bare foot on the floor and announced, "Now we must tell our healer the rest of the story, then we'll see if she can help with the clue. She is used to books and their ways. She gave Sapphire back her sight by looking at no more than three pages in her book of healing. She knows the words books use."

"I just used the index," Helen murmured. But she

wanted to hear the rest of the story, so she didn't protest too much. She was starting to hurt all over, from galloping, tunnelling and rolling about on hard rock. She needed to sit down.

In the glow of Lavender's flickering light balls, she could see a rounder, less jaggy rock against the wall of the cave so she headed towards it. She started to scramble up it, and was surprised when her foot sank in. She jerked her foot out, and fell backwards.

Yann laughed loudly. "That's not a stone, it's a mound of bat droppings!"

Lavender waved some light balls nearer, and Helen saw the rounded rock was a pile of grey ooze, covered in creatures with too many legs, or none at all. She hadn't smelt it earlier because of the smoke in her nostrils, but now she coughed, and moved away from the stinking heap. Yann was still laughing.

Helen suddenly felt completely alone. She was in a cold, damp, smelly cave, with unlikely beings who didn't entirely trust her and whom she didn't completely believe in. She hadn't had her tea, she was wet, bruised and smelt of smoke, and now she had bat jobby on one foot. She didn't really want to hear any more stories, she just wanted to go home.

Then the dragon, her chest rumbling softly, nudged a box towards Helen.

Lavender explained, "You can sit here, on this casket. Sapphire says she can trust you."

Helen looked at Rona with her deep brown eyes, Lavender with her cheeky smile, and Sapphire, glowing a beautiful seaside blue now she wasn't scared and sore. She might as well hear the next chapter of the story. She sat on the wooden casket with a padlock digging into her thigh, while the others settled down on shields or the rocky floor.

Yann had stopped laughing, and he stood straight and tall in front of Helen.

"You know so many of our secrets. So I will tell you some more."

Chapter 7

Yann filled the glimmering cave with his voice. "I will tell you what has happened since we took the Book two nights ago. The Book flew from us in fear, but Catesby and Sapphire fly faster than pages can, so they followed the Book under the clouds and over the hills to its first refuge.

"The Book flew into an old walled garden, at the base of a tall tower with no door. Young centaurs are told that long ago the garden belonged to a witch who imprisoned a human girl in the tower, but the girl escaped using her long golden pleat."

"Rapunzel!" exclaimed Helen.

"Yes, that's her name in our tales too. The witch, the girl and the prince are all gone now, but the witch's enchantments live on, and no one can enter the garden without permission. The Book knows all the answers, so it flew in easily. But none of us could follow.

"However, even her aunts admit that Lavender is a clever fairy. She spent all of the next day working on a spell, and last night she soothed the herbs in the garden and sent the enchantment to sleep.

"Last night, we thought that all we had to do was to find the Book, say we were sorry and take it back home. We didn't know that the dark creatures were trying to get the Book, so once Lavender had spoken to the herbs and checked the spell had worked, she went home, leaving me on my own."

Lavender swooped down to his right ear. "I'm so sorry. I wish I hadn't left you, Yann, but I did have to be back for a rehearsal of the Solstice dance. I would have been missed by my aunts if I had been late."

Yann held out his hand for the fairy and smiled at her. "You did your best, my friend. You let me in, that was all I asked you to do."

Yann spoke to Helen again. "Once she had gone, I leapt the wall myself.

"I started to look amongst the herbs and flowerbeds and bushes, and amongst the stones fallen over the years from the tower, hoping to find the Book. Then I saw a stone with words carved into it. But before I could read them, I heard hissing and growling, and a gang of creatures leapt on me from behind.

"To my shame, I did not wait to read the clue or try to lift the stone. I just fled. And as I leapt over the wall, I was bitten and ripped my own flesh by kicking the creature off.

"That is when I came to you, healer's child. I came for

your help because I could not admit to my own healers how I had been injured, and I could not face my friends with my failure." His voice was quiet, not ringing round the cave as it was when he laughed or told the brave parts of tales.

Rona stroked Yann's side. "It was not a failure. You found out lots we did not know. You discovered that the Master was also hunting the Book, that the Book had left us a riddle on a stone and that the stone was at the base of the tower. And if you hadn't been injured, we would never have met the healer's child." Rona turned to Helen.

"So tonight, we sent the largest and strongest amongst us, Sapphire, to pick up the stone riddle. But the Master must have sent more creatures, ones with more sense than teeth, and they waited until she was below the old tower, then knocked the loose stones and slates from the roof.

"But Sapphire carried the clue back with her, even when she could hardly see to fly. And now we shall read the riddle. Go and get your greatest treasure, Sapphire."

Sapphire went to her trove of glitter and sparkle, and picked up a brick-shaped grey stone. Helen saw that it had rough edges, and was about the size of a cat basket. On one of its largest sides, there were words chipped out in elegant straight lines. Sapphire brought the stone to Helen, and laid it at her feet.

Helen looked round at her companions, all waiting anxiously beside her. Then she read:

I come from a gap-toothed grin in the ground,
with no beginning and no end.

She looked back up. "What on earth does that mean?"

"It must be the clue from the Book. Can you help us unriddle it?" Rona pleaded.

"I haven't ever really done riddles. Is it another place you have to look?"

"It must be a clue leading to the place where the Book is now."

"But it seems to be about where it came from." Helen thought for a moment. "Did the Book come from the ground? From something that is like a grin in the ground?"

Rona said, "No, I don't think so. The Book has been with the fabled beasts since before humans moved from castles and farms to towns and cities. We learn from our elders that once upon a time, a wizard boasted that he knew everything in the world, and a tiny fairy challenged him to a duel, where they threw unanswerable questions at each other."

"Questions like what?" asked Helen.

"Questions like: Why is the sea salty when the rivers that fill it are sweet? How does a dragon brought up by eagles learn to breathe fire? Why is there no pink or brown in a rainbow? Where do midgies go when it rains? Why can you never be who your parents want you to be? What are wasps for? And, of course, why can't you tickle yourself?

"Soon the wizard and fairy were having so much fun that instead of fighting, they made it their life's work to collect all the questions in the world. They wrote them in shining gold ink in their Book; a Book bound in the bark from the very first silver birch tree and closed with a clasp made of pearls from the mermaids' gardens. They travelled the world, getting questions from every people: werewolves and sea serpents; naiads and dryads; babies in cradles and hermits on poles ... Then they wrote down the answers from their vast store of knowledge.

"Soon they had collected all the lore that helped our peoples survive and thrive. All the wisdom that kept us safe. They realized that the Book could be a tool to bind us together, but it could also be a weapon to destroy us.

"So when the wizard and fairy reached the end of their Book and the end of their lives, they gave the Book to all the fabled beasts together to keep safe. But they said that no one being was ever to be allowed to read the whole Book. That is why our ancestors drew up the rules of questioning. And that is why we should not have broken the rules."

Rona turned suddenly pale and sat down, her head in her hands.

Helen moved over to her and asked gently, "What kind of questions do you normally ask it?"

Rona lifted her smooth head. "We may ask about the balance of good and evil, or how to solve disputes between tribes and peoples, or how to survive in this new world. It contains much knowledge that would otherwise be lost as our tribes grow smaller."

Yann explained, "Long ago, when cities started to grow and railways started to cut up our world and humans seemed to be everywhere, the Book told us where we could live hidden and how we could travel concealed.

"And only in my grandfather's time, when the last of

the bronze generation of phoenixes died his last death too early after a lightning strike, the Book told us how to hatch the nest of copper phoenixes." He held his arm out to Catesby, who swooped down in a blaze of copper feathers and perched on his wrist. They grinned at each other.

Lavender added, "But the fabled beasts of this land do not keep the Book to themselves. Our brothers and sisters journey from all over our world to seek the Book's advice.

"Like when the sphinx sent a delegation from the desert, after she lost the answers to her riddles in a sandstorm. The Book advised her to close her eyes and let travellers through until she had woven new riddles.

"Or those English fairies whose nieces were turning their backs on the old magic and wishing to work only with rainbows. The Book said they would grow out of it, eventually."

Yann broke in, "But the Master has never sent to ask just one question at a Solstice Gathering. He does not want one answer, he wants many."

Helen frowned. "But what questions could he ask, that would have such terrible answers?"

Yann bent and stretched his bandaged leg. "He could ask for the potions to grow weasels the size of wolves and rats the size of cattle."

Rona added, "He could ask for charms to force the elders of the tribes to do his bidding rather than the best for their people."

Lavender whispered, "He could ask for the words to break through the magic protecting our sacred places."

Catesby squawked a comment that caused Rona to

gasp and Sapphire to send out a sudden hiccup of orange flame. Helen didn't ask for a translation.

Yann continued, "If the Master of the Maze has all the answers and follows none of the rules, and if no one else can ask the Book for help, he will soon have unlimited power over the fabled beasts. And he will not stop there." Yann came closer to Helen, and spoke quietly. "Soon he will look at your world and start using questions and answers to get round your magic too."

Helen shook her head. "We don't have magic."

"Yes, you do, you just call it science." Yann turned away and spoke into the emptiness of the cave. "The one question to which the Master craves the answer is: how can I rule this world?"

There was a cold dark silence.

Helen put her arm round Rona. She felt so warm and real. Helen had only just started truly believing in these people and their world, and now it might be destroyed.

"Alright then," Helen said firmly, "We'd better solve the riddle as fast as possible. Let's have another look.

I come from a gap-toothed grin in the ground,
with no beginning and no end.

"But the Book didn't come from a gap-toothed grin in the ground, did it?" she asked again.

"No," agreed Rona, "It is made of thick paper, ancient bark and sea pearls. From woods and water, not earth."

"So who is saying, 'I came from a gap-toothed grin in the ground' then?"

They all thought. Yann tapped a hoof. Catesby

preened his tail. Rona hummed a short melody over and over. Lavender went round the cave brightening up some balls of light. Sapphire rocked the stone back and forth with her clawed foot.

Helen watched them all. She watched the words on the stone, and the moving shadows the stone cast on the bumpy floor.

"The stone!" she cried out. "The stone is saying: 'I came from a gap-toothed grin in the ground.' It's a place where stones make a shape without beginning or end!"

She closed her eyes, seeing shapes and patterns made out of stones in her head. Towers and cliffs, sheepfolds and cairns, harbours and mazes. But they all had beginnings and ends. They all had tops, bottoms, doors and corners. None of them seemed to answer the riddle. Suddenly, she thought of a shape that had no beginning nor end, that just kept going round and round and round ...

"A circle! A stone circle! That's a shape without end. And standing stones in a circle ... you know, those huge ancient stones poking up out of the earth ... they look just like teeth in an open mouth. They could be a gap-toothed grin. It must be an old stone circle!"

Yann was looking at her with surprise on his face. Lavender blew her a kiss. Rona smiled at her confidently and said, "I knew you were the one to help. A human bard with books in her blood! Which stone circle could it be?"

Yann grunted. "Sapphire, you're the expert on stones. Where does this rock come from?"

Sapphire sat back on her hind legs and picked the

stone up between her front legs. She turned it over and looked at each of its six sides. Then she sighed a breath of pale smoke and snuffed a small dragon laugh. She laid the stone on the rough floor, with the writing downwards, and tapped her tiniest silver claw on a mark on the top surface.

Helen brushed shoulders with Rona as they all leaned forward to look.

Scratched on to the stone was a shape like a tree with three short branches pointing up on one side, and four on the other.

"A rune!" exclaimed Yann. "Well done. Can you read it?"

Sapphire snorted again, and rumbled briefly.

Yann said disapprovingly, "It's a joke! It says 'ouch!' Sapphire says she thinks someone dropped the stone on his foot and scratched an 'ouch' rune. The Book wouldn't tell jokes. It must have been on the stone before the Book carved its clue."

"But that's great," said Helen, "We want to know where the stone came from, so if the rune is earlier than the Book's visit to the garden then it's a really good clue. I can look for a book about stone circles at school tomorrow if you want, see if any circles near here have runes carved on the stones.

"Then we can meet tomorrow night, and I might be able to tell you which circle this stone came from. And if you think it would be helpful, maybe I could come with you again, just in case you need my first aid kit."

Sapphire mumbled something warmly, which Rona explained was an offer to carry the human who had restored her sight anywhere, anytime. Helen grinned.

Her Dad always said the first song she'd ever written, when she was six, was about a ride on a dragon. "Thank you so much, I would love that."

"But not tonight," said Yann. "Sapphire, you need to recover and regain your strength for tomorrow. I will take the healer's child home safely, and we will all meet again in her garden tomorrow after the sun goes down. We have only three days before the Winter Solstice, when our elders will notice the loss of the Book."

Suddenly the group broke up. Lavender's lights dimmed and everyone said goodbye. Yann took Helen home through the wider front entrance to Sapphire's cave. He cantered rather than galloped, but he did not say one word to her the whole way home.

When he let her down in front of the garage, she asked him politely to step back in so she could check his wound. She unwound the bandages, and tried not to sound too surprised when she said, "It seems to be healing perfectly, no pus or swelling at all." She put a clean pad on and bound it up again.

He barely seemed to hear her, or notice the new bandage. But just as he left, he turned to her.

"Human girl. I hope you find the answer to our riddle soon, because the Master's creatures have been in the walled garden since last night and they will have read the clue long before we did. We have to puzzle out the answer, then reach the stone circle and the Book before they do, or the Master will gain answers to all the questions he burns with, and we fabled beasts will have no answers at all."

Helen asked, "Are you afraid of that, Yann, even though you're not afraid of pain?"

"Yes, I am afraid." He looked directly into her eyes. "I am afraid because it will mean war. A war my people cannot win, and a war your people may lose too."

Then he galloped off.

Chapter 8

Helen woke full of excitement and jumped eagerly out of bed. If she could find the right stone circle today, she would fly there tonight on a dragon!

After buttoning up her school dress, she stood in front of the mirror pulling her thick dark curls into a ponytail. Then she turned to go downstairs for breakfast, and nearly tripped over the green first aid kit in the middle of the floor, where she'd dropped it on arriving home last night in her rush to get cleaned up before suppertime.

The rucksack was slightly scorched and very dirty. She couldn't possibly put it back in her Mum's surgery. She would have to replace it. But first she would have to refill it with supplies she might need tonight: a new syringe, more saline, swabs, clean bandages and what else? What could go wrong at a stone circle? What injuries could her new friends suffer? She tried not to think of huge stone slabs falling on small fairies, or even middle-sized schoolgirls.

She shoved the first aid kit under her bed and went downstairs for breakfast.

Nicola wasn't being a horse today. Today she was being a teddy's mummy, feeding porridge to a bright pink bear in a bib. "Open wiiiiiiiiide!" she said to the bear. Helen gave her little sister a kiss, and got a dollop of porridge on her sleeve in thanks.

Her Dad handed Helen a bowl of porridge, and waved vaguely at the blueberries and honey on the table.

"Mr Crombie phoned last night to make an appointment for his cat's booster jags. He seemed a bit worried about this solo you're supposed to be performing at the concert. He says you still haven't told him which piece you're going to play yet. Is that right?"

Oops, thought Helen, I should have been looking for a tune last night, not crawling about in caves and solving riddles.

"I just haven't played it for him yet, Dad, that's all. It'll be ready by Monday. Don't worry."

"Look ... Mum and I know you want to be a great fiddle player, but we're still not sure about this summer school idea. It's a lot of work, and if you aren't ready to find, practise and perform a solo, then perhaps you should just wait a year or two."

"But I can't wait! These particular violinists might only play together at next year's summer school, and then maybe never again. I may never get this chance again."

Helen's Dad tried to look stern. "Then you need to impress Mr Crombie at his rehearsals, don't you, rather than make him nervous about his concert?"

"I know, I know." Helen wanted to distract her Dad from this awkward conversation, so she asked, "Dad, do you know anything about stone circles?"

"What ... like Stonehenge? That sort of thing?"

"Yes. Are there any round here?"

Her Dad thought. "I don't know of any standing stones nearby. There are a couple of very old burial sites and lots of Roman remains in the Borders, but the big circles are mostly in the south of England, I think. There are a couple in Orkney and the Western Isles though. Why do you ask?"

"Just something I read." Helen grinned, remembering reading the riddle on the stone in the flickering light of the cave.

Then her Mum marched in, slightly grumpy, as she often was until she'd had her breakfast.

"I've lost my first aid kit. The rucksack I use for long distance jobs like sheep on cliff faces, and puppies in septic tanks. The one in the Landrover has just fallen apart, and I can't find my spare anywhere. Does anyone know where it is?"

Helen didn't know *exactly* where the rucksack had come to rest under her bed when she pushed it with her foot, so she crossed her fingers and said, "I don't know, Mum." Then she filled her mouth with blueberry porridge and started eating very fast.

"Alasdair, do you know where it is?"

"No, Tricia dear. Where did you last see it?"

"It's usually filled with supplies and hanging on the door of the small animal surgery, but it's not there."

"Did you take it with you to rescue the sheep a couple of nights ago?"

"No, it was that barbed wire which wrecked my old one."

"Nicola, have you taken Mummy's green bag?" Dad asked gently.

"Green bag for picnic. Teddy bear picnic."

"Nicola! That's Mummy's ..." her Mum's voice started to rise.

Helen broke in, "No, Mum!" She didn't want Nicola taking the blame for her nighttime adventures again. "No, Mum, Nicola doesn't mean *your* green bag. Remember she has a wee green bag with flowers on it, and she uses it for pretend shopping and picnics. That's the bag she means. I'm sure she wouldn't mind if you borrowed it though, for your plasters and stuff."

"It's got much more important equipment in it than plasters and stuff, as you would know, young lady, if you ever paid the slightest attention to what I do for a living."

"I don't have to pay attention, Mum, I don't want to be a vet. I want to be a musician."

"For which you will have to practise a bit more," reminded her Dad. Feeling got at from both sides, Helen put her half-finished bowl of porridge in the sink and clomped off to pack her school bag.

Helen didn't get a chance to sneak into the school library until lunchtime. As soon as she had finished her packed lunch, she went into the oldest part of the school, which had once been the original village hall. It wasn't used for teaching any more and she noticed that it was starting to smell quite musty. The library was much bigger than her classroom. There were lots of old books on high wooden shelves, and a ladder on wheels to reach them, but the books that the pupils usually needed were easier to reach, on grey metal bookcases in the middle of the room.

Helen searched the history and geography shelves and found several books on stone circles and other Neolithic remains from four or five thousand years ago.

She was dismayed to discover that there were hundreds of stone circles, stone rows and standing stones in Britain, but then she remembered that she was looking for a shape without end, so she limited her search to circles.

Stonehenge was the most obvious circle, but a photo in a recent book showed it surrounded by barriers and cameras, so it would be hard to get into, even at night, even with the help of a dragon. She had to hope that the Book's clue came from another, less touristy, circle.

She picked up an old book with yellow crinkled pages containing sketches of stone circles. She flicked through it, back to front, as she always did with serious books, hoping to get to the good bits fast without having to read the introduction.

As the sketches passed her in a cartoon blur of stones moving and dancing, one shape caught her eye. She stopped flicking and turned back half a dozen pages to find the picture that had leapt out at her.

She saw a huge stone circle, a perfect, beautiful circle, even though there were gaps where some stones had fallen.

It was called the Ring of Brodgar, and was on the mainland of Orkney, the group of islands just off the very top corner of Scotland. But what Helen had noticed was the small sketch in the corner of the page; a drawing of just one of the massive stones. It had a rune carved on it, in the same branched tree style as the rune on Sapphire's block. The notes underneath said a smaller stone with a rune on it had gone missing from Brodgar years ago.

"We could take it back to Brodgar tonight!" she said out loud, delighted to have solved the riddle.

Helen glanced quickly through the rest of the book, but there was no other circle that answered the riddle. So she returned to the Ring of Brodgar, and copied the layout of the circle, including the deep ditch round it and the lochs either side of it, into a notebook she'd brought from home.

She was just sliding all the books back into their spaces when the bell rang for the end of lunchtime. She ran down the corridor between the old building and the new classrooms. As she turned the corner and pushed open the heavy fire door, she heard a noise behind her. She whirled round quickly, and saw something vanish round the corner. It looked like a tail, not at floor level, but at the height of Helen's waist. She'd been the only person in the library and there were only storerooms in this corridor. So who else was here? Helen stood still and listened. In the background she heard the shuffling and chatter of classes filing back in, but nearby she thought she heard breathing. Rasping, gasping breathing.

She clenched her fists and thought about Yann running away from creatures with teeth. She took a step back towards the library, but then heard Mrs Murray shout from the new building.

"Helen Strang! Get to your class this minute."

Helen called, "Yes Miss," and ran into the bright light, straight to her classroom.

There was no rehearsal after school on Wednesday, so Helen was back home while it was still light. Her Mum was at a conference at Edinburgh University, and her Dad had taken Nicola swimming in Selkirk, so she had the house to herself for an hour.

First, she restocked the first aid kit, adding a few extra bandages and swabs just to be safe.

Then, remembering how hungry she had been by the end of the cave adventure, she made some sandwiches. She didn't know what her new friends ate, so she chose for them: cheese, tuna, chicken and jam. She wondered what horses would like, and added some salad leaves to the plastic box too. Finally, she hid the rucksack and the sandwiches in a bush by the back fence.

As the sun sank lower, her Dad and Nicola came back smelling of chlorine. Helen sat in her room with her music books and tried – yet again – to find a short violin piece that she felt was perfect for her. She had been enjoying herself too much these past few days to play anything sad, and none of the bouncy pieces were serious enough for someone who was trying to save the world from an evil Minotaur.

She found an old book of traditional Scottish dance tunes that Mr Crombie had lent her and was playing her way through those when she suddenly realized that it was almost dark outside. She put her fiddle in its case, ran downstairs and grabbed her fleece.

She trotted through the kitchen, where her Dad was blowing Nicola's nose.

"I heard you playing upstairs, it sounded great," he said smiling.

"That was just a warm up. I should really go out to the garage now, to try some more complex music for my solo. I've made some sandwiches, so don't worry if I'm not back for a while."

Helen had thought about her words carefully, and was pretty sure she hadn't actually lied. She should indeed be practising in the garage, and she really had made sandwiches ... and she certainly wouldn't be back for a while.

So she gave her Dad a big kiss, and jumped out of the way of a huge sneeze from her little sister. Then she bounced out of the back door and ran to the garage. She nipped in just long enough to put her fiddle carefully on the couch, and switch on the light so it shone through the dusty windows. From the house, it would look as if she was still there.

She headed for the darkest part of the garden where she found Yann resting on the ground with his legs folded under him, and Rona leaning on his flank, her legs stretched out on the grass.

Rona grinned at Helen. "Was that you playing? It was lovely."

Helen smiled shyly. "I was just sight-reading, trying to find a new piece to play at my school concert."

"Enough chatter, girls," said Yann grandly, springing to his hooves. "We have work to do. The others are in the wood up the hill. We must join them."

"I made food." Helen grabbed the box and rucksack from behind the bush. "You can eat while I tell you what I found."

So, as they sat round a tree stump in the old birch wood above the house, Rona ate tuna sandwiches, Yann ate all the salad, Lavender ate little bits of jam sandwiches and Catesby pecked at the fairy's crusts. Sapphire delicately nibbled the chicken sandwiches.

"You'd really have preferred a whole chicken, wouldn't you?" laughed Helen.

Then she passed round her notebook so they could all see the sketches.

"The most likely stone circle for our riddle is the Ring of Brodgar on the main island of Orkney, just off the north coast. It's a huge circle, with almost thirty stones still standing, and at least one of the standing stones has runes carved on it. Also a stone went missing from there years ago, and it had a rune on it too. So we could take the stone home, and find your Book at the same time. The only problem is, how do we get there? It's about 250 miles north of here."

Sapphire grunted quietly. Perhaps she didn't want to roar and set the trees on fire. Rona explained, "Sapphire will fly us. She can fly you and me on her back, Catesby can keep up with us and Lavender can perch on our shoulders."

Yann said slowly, "But I can't go, can I?" He stamped a hoof, and spoke angrily. "I can't really fit on Sapphire's back, not for that long, and even at a gallop I won't get to Caithness tonight. And the currents in the Pentland Firth are too strong for me to swim anyway. I can't go. The human girl can go, but I can't."

Rona patted his withers. "No, you can't come this time, but you *can* go home, and help prepare for the Gathering and keep our people from worrying about where we are. If all of us are missing every night this week, they will start to think we are up to something."

"So I go home and do housework, while you face danger and find the Book?"

"Have you found out about those teeth yet?" asked Helen, "The teeth of the creature that bit you? You thought that might be useful." Yann humphed and turned his back on her.

She tried again. "I think I was being watched at school today, by something with a tail, something that breathed in a raspy way. Perhaps you could spend some time working out what is watching us. That would be more useful than sulking, for example."

He swung back towards her. "I wasn't sulking. I was thinking."

Lavender swooped down and pointed her tiny finger at Yann's nose. "I had to practise synchronized spells while you leapt into the walled garden. You can go and help stamp out the dance floor while we go island hopping. It's only fair."

So Yann agreed to go home, to be seen helping with

the Gathering preparations, and to work out what creatures the Master was using.

Helen grabbed the last few cheese sandwiches, and watched a drooping Yann walk off through the trees. Then she put the rucksack on her back and joined the others at the edge of the wood. Sapphire had lowered her belly to the ground, and was holding out her front leg as a step. The dragon was clutching the grey riddle rock in her silver claws. Rona climbed on, sat between Sapphire's neck and wings and beckoned Helen to join her.

Thinking of all the dragon rides she had dreamt of as a child, and wondering if this was real, Helen put her foot gently on Sapphire's leg and held onto the dragon's slender silver spikes to pull herself high up behind Rona.

Sapphire certainly felt real. In dreams dragons felt like couches or bikes, comfy and safe. But Sapphire was too wide to sit on comfortably, her scales were bumpy and poky, and as she took a single lurching step forward, Helen nearly fell off. She grabbed onto the nearest dragon spike and held on tight.

Rona turned round anxiously. "Are you alright?"

"I think so." Helen laughed. "I've never done this when I've been awake before!"

Then Sapphire took one more clumsy step and leapt into the air. Helen couldn't see how something so solid could possibly fly, but with a couple of powerful beats of her huge blue-grey wings Sapphire was high in the air and moving forward at great speed.

"Go north!" Helen yelled. "Just go north until we see the sea!"

Chapter 9

Helen found it easier to balance on the dragon when she was in the air. The smooth beats of Sapphire's wings didn't swing her from side to side like the dragon's lurching footsteps did, so once Helen got used to the feel of the dragon's muscles stretching and contracting under her, and the pressure of the air forced down by the wings at each beat, she felt quite secure.

Sapphire didn't have a completely spiky back, just half a dozen pairs of spikes spaced along her spine, and the girls sat between them, using them as handles. Helen's grip on the silver spikes in front of her was soon light and gentle, not tight and white-knuckled.

There was a longer pair of spikes on Sapphire's head, and a cluster of smaller ones, like a medieval weapon, on her tail. She had gleaming blue scales, shining in the moonlight. The scales on her legs and neck were quite small, but on her back they were as big as Helen's hand.

The smooth, dry scales were leaf-shaped, and fitted neatly together in clusters and rows. Helen thought she could glimpse patterns and shapes in the scales ... clouds, crystals, spirals and feathers.

The wind whizzed past them, carrying the occasional surprise, like a shocked and swerving owl, or a sudden slap of cold wet cloud.

Helen cried out the first time she was surrounded by tiny swirling drops of water, and then laughed with relief a moment later as they flew on, leaving the cloud behind. This was nothing like dragon dreams or dragon stories; it was much, much better!

For most of the journey, Lavender sat on Helen's shoulder, holding onto her hair, whispering in her ear and giggling, which was quite tickly. Catesby flew above them, keeping up comfortably with the dragon and her passengers.

After they had flown for so long that most of the stars had come out, Sapphire swooped down through a layer of cloud and landed beside a wall of huge flagstones shoved into the bare earth. Helen and Rona slid to the ground, and Catesby glided down beside them. Lavender perched on Sapphire's snout, a safe distance from her nostrils.

But the wind that had battered them as they flew, which Helen had thought was caused by their speed through the air, didn't die down much as they landed. They took shelter behind the wall, so they could hear each other, and Lavender lit a few light balls, which she kept near the wall so they wouldn't blow away.

"This is Caithness," Lavender explained to Helen as Sapphire rumbled. "The last land in Scotland before the Pentland Firth. Now we need to decide how to get to the right island, and what we will do when we get there."

Helen wished she had brought a map of Scotland as well as the sketch of the stone circle she had shown them earlier.

"Have any of you been to Orkney?" she asked.

"I have," said Rona, "but I went by sea. The islands shouldn't be too hard to find. We'll listen for waves on rocks and the sound of seabirds, or we could just ask for directions."

Catesby squawked briefly and Rona explained, "Catesby thinks we shouldn't land inside the circle, in case the Master's creatures are already there. We should land a little way off and sneak up to the circle."

Helen didn't like to ask whether dragons can sneak, especially dragons carrying rocks. Instead she asked, "Are we looking for a clue or for your Book?"

"Both. If the Book is there, we treat it with great respect and ask it to return with us. If it has been scared off again and has left a clue, we grab the clue and get away as quickly as possible."

"And if the Master or his creatures are there?" Lavender's voice wobbled a little.

"Then we still have to get the Book or the clue. By force, cunning or sacrifice if need be," Rona said grimly.

Lavender nodded, "Then we must decide where to look."

Glancing at Helen's sketch, the fairy drew the stone circle on the bare earth with her tiny toe. She jumped into the middle. "I will search the centre, as that is where the power of the circle is concentrated. And the rest of you must look at each stone on the edge, including the gaps where stones have fallen or been taken, as there will still be energy in their emptiness."

From her position in the centre, she split the circle into four quadrants and gave each of her friends an equal stretch of the edge to search.

They agreed to split up outside the circle, and return as quickly and quietly as possible to their landing site once they had explored their quadrant.

Helen's tummy, which hadn't objected to dragon swoops and swings, was starting to somersault at the thought of searching for a stone circle in the dark, on her own. It had been exciting hearing the tales of the others' adventures and patching them up afterwards, but now she was inside the adventure, putting herself at risk, facing barely understood dangers to find something she had never seen. However, she could hardly back out now, miles from home and so close to the circle.

As they climbed back on to Sapphire in the fading fairy light, Helen noticed that Rona had a small fur fabric bag on her back. "Is that to carry the Book home in? Because we could use my rucksack if you like."

"No, this is my skin. If we find what we need without meeting danger or anyone getting hurt, I may go and visit my cousins off Stromness before we leave. I need my skin to return to my real seal shape."

Helen hesitated before sitting down behind Rona. That bag was real fur. More than that, it was real living fur. It was part of Rona's body that she put on and off.

Rona seemed the most normal of Helen's new friends; no wings, only two legs, no fire-breathing. But Helen suddenly realized that Rona was probably the strangest of them all; Rona changed shape.

"Does it hurt, changing shape?"

"It's a bit stretchy and itchy and quite tiring, but it's not sore. However, I do have to take good care of my seal skin. I have to keep it with me or else leave it with someone I trust completely, because if I lose it I can never swim or sing in the sea again ..."

Then Sapphire leapt off into the dark air, and the speed of her flight into the wind dragged the rest of Rona's words right past Helen's ears.

Helen had no idea how they found the mainland of Orkney. They flew north for a few more minutes, until they were surrounded by the sound and smell of the sea. Then Sapphire circled round and flew so close to the tops of the waves that they were splashed by the salty spray thrown up by the gathering wind.

Rona called out a question in a strange, shrieky voice and some seals answered her, heads rising out of the churning sea. Rona pointed Sapphire in a new direction, and soon they could see a faint glow of light from towns on the edges of the islands.

They swerved round a burning flare from an oil terminal on one of the smaller islands, and found themselves above the sand, rocks and fields of the Orkney mainland. Seals resting by a rusting pier gave Rona further directions to the circle.

They found the ring a couple of miles inland, on a small hill between two lochs, just beside a narrow road.

From above, the stones looked like great slabs of

darkness in the night. Sapphire landed gently and silently at the side of the road, between the larger loch and the circle. Catesby and Lavender perched on fence posts. Rona slid down off the dragon, then Helen followed her. They huddled together.

"Off we go, each to their own search," instructed Lavender.

And everyone but Helen moved away.

Lavender and Catesby flew off silently. Rona climbed over the fence, jogged through the long waving grass towards the circle and was quickly lost in the darkness. Helen's question about whether dragons could sneak was answered when she realized that Sapphire had vanished from her side too.

The light of the moon and stars was just enough to see the circle ahead, over a flimsy gate and a gentle rise of uneven grass and heather.

She couldn't see or hear anything move, neither friend nor foe. She didn't know what the foes would look like or sound like anyway. She didn't have any idea what a clue from a Book would look like either. If it was carved on a huge stone, she wouldn't be able to take it away with her, though she could scribble the words in the notebook tucked in her fleece pocket.

Helen still hadn't moved.

She had to do this now, or Lavender would soon be back from her search of the centre.

She took a deep breath and forced herself to put her right foot forward. Pushing her way against the wind and her own fear, Helen clambered quickly over the fence and the rough ground towards the circle. She could see gaps where half the stones had fallen or were missing, but it was still an amazing sight. Nearly thirty massive stones jutted up to the sky; the only solid things unmoved by the wind swirling round the island.

The circle was on a slope, so the lower stones, nearest to Helen, were harder to see, but the ones on the top edge were outlined clearly against the grey sky and the stars.

She was safe so far, and seemed to be alone, which was scary. But alone was better than being surrounded by evil creatures with teeth and dark powers. Suddenly the ground fell away from her and she pitched forwards into emptiness. Was this a pit; a trap dug by the Master's creatures? For a moment she panicked, then realized it must be the ditch round the stones. She rolled down to the bottom, with heather scratching her but also catching her and breaking her fall.

Helen shook her head. She should have been more careful. She'd known about the ditch, and had even sketched it in the library. She didn't bother standing up, just scrambled straight up the steep side of the ditch to the stones above.

Helen had been asked to search the quadrant of stones nearest their landing place. When she reached the first stone in her section, she patted its base and the grass around it with her hands, feeling for books or bricks, stones or jigsaw puzzles ... whatever the clue might be. She ran her hands over the grainy stone surfaces of its front and back face, reaching high over her head to feel for any recent carving. But all she felt were patches of lichen and rough cracks.

She did the same with the second stone a few paces away. It was only a shattered stump, with layers of rock splitting apart like the pages of a slightly open book. Helen knelt beside it and poked her fingers cautiously into each space. She found nothing but cold and darkness.

The third standing stone in her search was one of the tallest in the whole circle, which towered over her as she walked towards it and began to run her hands over it. Suddenly, she heard a small scream carried on the wind. It sounded like Lavender and was coming from the centre of the circle.

She turned towards the sound of the scream and, as she did so, she tripped over something stuck in the ground at the base of the stone and fell full length on the hard ground. She reached back and touched something taller than it was wide, pointing up to the sky just like the stones, but not much bigger than Helen's foot. She tugged it out of the earth, shoved it in her fleece pocket and ran towards the circle's centre.

As Helen ran, the noise from the centre grew louder and more confused. Lavender's high-pitched screams were joined by other screeches and squawks that Helen couldn't identify, though they reminded her, bizarrely, of holidays at the seaside.

The blackness in the centre began to glow and glimmer. Helen recognized balls of fairy light from Lavender's wand, moving crazily in the wind, and sparks and small flames from Sapphire's throat. The others must be gathering there too, to help Lavender. And Helen would join the fight just as soon as she got there.

But suddenly, in the flickering light, she saw a sight that stopped her breath and her feet. She saw all her friends in a group round a pile of small stones. Lavender and Catesby were flying above the stones, Rona and Sapphire were on the ground, all hitting out at large white birds that were attacking them. But high above their heads, unnoticed by any of them, was a huge green net held in the beaks of dozens more birds.

Helen saw the danger at once and yelled, "Run! Scatter!" Before her friends could move, there was a sudden flurry as all the attacking birds flew away from the fight and the net was dropped. Rona, Sapphire, Lavender and Catesby were trapped.

Lavender was so tiny that after being knocked to the ground by the net, she was able to fly through one of the diamond-shaped holes and escape, but she was immediately mobbed by the birds, which Helen now recognised as massive grey and white seagulls. The fairy weaved and danced through the air to avoid their beaks and claws.

Rona, Catesby and Sapphire were struggling in the green plastic net. Catesby's wings were poking through the holes, but he couldn't squeeze his body out, and Sapphire was roaring and twisting and getting her spikes tied in knots. Then the dragon took a deep breath and sent a jet of white hot flame onto the net.

Parts of the net vanished instantly but Rona screamed. Drops of molten plastic had landed on her bare arm.

Helen was crouched in the heather, hoping the seagulls wouldn't see her, and rummaging in her rucksack. Most of the birds were swooping above the net, pecking at their captives, and beating them with their wings. Sapphire blasted more flame into the mass of wings, and blew many of the seagulls, scorched and screaming, up into the sky. There was a sudden stink of burnt feathers.

Most of the seagulls flapped off to join the flock trying to catch Lavender as she zigzagged round the stones. She was fast and nimble enough to escape the seagulls, but the wind kept catching her and blowing her back at them.

Sapphire kept twisting, tangling herself further and knocking Rona off her feet.

"Stop!" yelled Helen. "Stop struggling and stay still." She had found a large scalpel in the bag and started to hack away at the thick strands of salty net, which still had bits of seaweed and fish scales embedded in it.

First she freed Rona, who was sobbing and holding her arm, but who immediately ran off to call encouragement to Lavender and urge her to fly down to the ground.

As Helen started to slice through the net round Catesby, she was whacked in the back by a force so strong that she fell forward onto the phoenix.

She whirled round to see a seagull flying straight at her head. She ducked, but it wheeled round and flew at her again. Its webbed feet scraped her shoulder this time, ripping her fleece. As she shoved it away with her elbow, it lunged for her face, the yellow beak so close that she could see the red dot on its sharp lower half as the hooked upper half tried to gouge into her eyes.

Seagulls were such common birds; she had never noticed just how *huge* they were, nor how sharp and long their beaks were, nor what terrifying birds they could be if you were their prey.

Helen was shouting and stabbing at the bird with her scalpel when Sapphire roared. Helen guessed it was a warning or an instruction, and flung herself down on the ground, hands over her head. She felt a whoosh of hot air, and the gull screamed. There was the smell of barbecue, then silence.

Helen sat up, said, "Thank you," to Sapphire, and started calmly cutting through the net again. She didn't look round to see what had happened to the gull.

It took just a moment to free Catesby and then she tried to cut the confusion of plastic woven round the dragon. She was careful not to slash through the beaded necklace the dragon still wore on her front leg. Helen managed to cut the net away from Sapphire's head and legs, and free her wings, but the knots of trailing plastic round her spikes would just have to wait.

When she had let everyone go, Helen looked up to see if Lavender had escaped the gang of seagulls. The squawking and yelling had moved away from the circle and was now over the nearest loch. Helen could see the occasional glow of light from Lavender's wand. She picked up the first aid kit, ran past the lower stones, slid through the ditch and flung herself over the fence, heading for the water. Sapphire and Catesby had taken to the air, Sapphire to drive off the rest of the seagulls from the circle with her huge leathery wings and brief jets of flame, Catesby to join Rona in trying to rescue Lavender.

But as Helen rushed across the road, she heard a small scream, a chorus of triumphant squawks and then a tiny splash.

She reached the water's edge just as Sapphire landed beside her. There was no sign of Rona or the fairy. Catesby, chattering his beak in agitation, was clearly telling the dragon what had happened, but Helen had no idea what he was saying. Sapphire took off again to scatter the swarm of seagulls over the loch, and in the light from her fire, Helen saw a round shiny head break through the loch's surface a couple of hundred yards from the shore. Was it a seal? Could it be Rona? Then she saw a long pale arm rise out of the water too, and a voice called faintly, "I've got her."

Helen was relieved that Rona was still a girl. Perhaps she could explain what was going on. The selkie was swimming quickly and smoothly, but with one hand always clear of the water.

"I've got her," she repeated as she neared the shore, "but she isn't breathing. I think she's drowned. I think she's dead."

Chapter 10

Rona held the motionless fairy close to her chest as she emerged from the loch.

"Give her to me, now!" demanded Helen. She took the sodden handful of fairy from Rona, then realized she could hardly see her. Lavender was the one who had lit all their adventures so far. Helen turned to Sapphire as she landed on the shore and asked, "Can you give me some light without burning me?"

Sapphire opened her mouth wide and produced a pale yellow glow from deep in her throat.

Helen examined Lavender. Her dress was dark with water and her hair was stuck to her head. Her face was white and her eyes were closed. She was freezing cold, and totally limp. Helen didn't think there was a spark of life in the fairy, until she saw that her right hand was still gripping her wand.

Helen pushed the rucksack at Rona. "Open it and find some dry bandages."

Helen knelt on the ground, using Sapphire's body to shelter her from the wind. Then she used one precious breath to blow her own hair off her sweaty forehead, and used the next one to blow, ever so softly, into Lavender's mouth and nose. Putting her lips in a tiny pout over the fairy's face, she blew in a gentle rhythm. After five breaths, she stopped and pressed a fingertip five times to the fairy's chest to try to start her heart. Then she breathed into her again.

Rona held out a ripped square of bandage. Helen wrapped the fairy in the fabric and rubbed her gently to warm her up. Then she continued breathing and pressing, pressing and breathing.

Rona was weeping behind her, but Helen had to concentrate on counting, and breathing and pressing. She could cry later if she had to.

Suddenly, as Helen was pressing her chest for the third cycle, Lavender coughed. Helen tipped her hand to hold the fairy upright and gave her face a wipe with the bandage.

Lavender coughed again, and opened her eyes. She tried to speak, but instead she spat water onto Helen's sleeve.

"Ooops, sorry," she croaked.

Helen couldn't speak to say it was alright. She was just amazed that this drowned little fairy was alive in her hands and being so polite.

Rona whispered over her shoulder, "You brought her back to life. You can do healing magic of your own."

Then Catesby squawked. Rona nodded, "Catesby says that those scavenging outlaws were trying to trap us in the stone circle for someone, and that we had better get out of here before that someone arrives."

Helen swaddled the damp fairy in a dry bandage and held her carefully in her hands as she clambered back on Sapphire.

"We will fly to a safe distance and work out what to do next," said Rona as Sapphire took off from the loch shore.

Helen looked down as Sapphire gained height over the circle. She couldn't see anything but blackness in the middle, though the moonlight showed some of the tall grey stones now streaked with scorch marks.

As they flew over the smaller loch, the wind died down for a moment and they heard a deep, resonating roar of anger from the stone circle behind them. Helen shivered and so did the fairy cupped in her hands.

Sapphire's wings beat even faster, heading straight for a dip in the hills of a large island to the south, taking them out of sight and hearing of whoever was in the circle. Once they were through the valley, they landed on a long curved beach covered with huge rounded rocks. The cliffs and hills surrounding the bay sheltered them from the driving wind.

Rona looked round. "I've seen this beach from the sea. It's Rackwick Bay on Hoy. We should be safe here."

So while Helen, Rona, and Catesby each perched on a massive pebble, and Sapphire balanced her weight over three, Lavender told her story from the safety of Helen's arms. The fairy's voice grew stronger as she warmed up and dried out.

"I found that pile of stones in the centre of the circle

and thought it might mark the clue, so I tried to crawl into it in case the riddle was inside, but it wasn't. Then I tried to dig under it in case the riddle was buried, but it wasn't. And then I thought maybe the cairn *was* the clue, so I tried to memorize how the stones were placed so we could read them later. I was concentrating so hard that when something dived at me and picked me up in its claws I forgot myself completely and screamed. I'm so sorry. I lured you all into a trap, away from the standing stones so they could drop the net on us."

Rona shook her head. "It wasn't your fault. Thanks to Sapphire melting the net and Helen cutting it, we got out of the trap. But we nearly lost you, Lavender, and we didn't get the Book or the clue. Perhaps the Master already has it."

"He can't have, or else why would he be trying to catch us. If he had the Book, he wouldn't be bothering with us." Lavender coughed.

Rona said firmly, "This has gone far enough. I know I said we would get the Book by force or cunning or sacrifice, but I didn't realize what that meant. You nearly died, Lavender. We have to tell our parents. We have to let them use their magic and skills and knowledge to find the Book. We just can't do it ourselves."

Catesby squawked but Rona didn't bother to translate for Helen, she just snapped back, "Well, Yann isn't here, and Yann didn't hold Lavender's lifeless body in his hands."

"But I am still alive," Lavender pointed out. "As long as we have Helen, we have survived everything the Master has thrown at us. I think we should keep trying."

"So far the Master has merely thrown weasels, rocks

and seagulls at us, but we've been damaged every time. I think he can get nastier if he has to, and I'm not sure that Helen's green bag holds much more magic. Anyway we can't keep trying, because we have nothing to go on. The Book is either in the Master's hands, or it has fled and we have no clue to tell us where it has gone. We must go home now and confess what we have done."

Helen thought Rona might be right, that telling their parents might be the best plan, but she couldn't keep her triumph to herself any longer.

"Actually, we do have something to go on. I think I might have found the clue."

They all turned to look at her, four very different heads, but all with gleaming eyes and slightly open mouths.

"I didn't get to the centre of the circle as fast as the rest of you when Lavender screamed because I tripped over something, at the base of the third stone. Here it is."

She pulled the object from her pocket. It felt smooth and almost warm. She brushed the dry earth from one end.

"It's driftwood."

It was light, as driftwood always is, like the sea had washed all the substance out of the wood and left nothing but the shape. It was pale and clean on one side, but when Helen turned it over, she saw tiny marks burnt dark into the wood on the other side.

"I think this is the clue."

They all crowded onto Helen's rock and peered at the tiny words, Lavender's flickering light balls jostling for space between their heads. Helen read slowly:

Here there is great change and fear:
Writhing snake to bar of hot iron,
Slippery newt to growling bear.
If you can hold strong and fast,
You will hold me in your hands at last.

Rona repeated it in a sing song voice.

Helen said, "Bits of that sound familiar. Like it's from a song I once heard, or a story my Gran used to tell me."

"We're all too tired to think about it just now." Rona yawned. "We can show it to Yann when we get back to Clovenshaws."

"To Yann?" said Lavender archly. "Not to your mummy and daddy?"

"No. Helen has given us one last chance. If we can work this out and get the Book tomorrow, without putting ourselves at risk again, then perhaps we can avoid letting them know how stupid we have been."

Sapphire grunted, and Catesby nodded in agreement.

Rona turned to Helen, "They're going to watch for the Master's creatures leaving Orkney. We don't want to leave at the same time and meet over the Pentland Firth."

The two winged friends took off and headed into the darkness, leaving Rona, Helen and Lavender on the rocky beach. Rona hugged her knees up to her chest, and then winced.

Helen asked, "Is your arm sore?"

Rona stretched her arm out to Helen, and Lavender handed Helen her wand. "Keep using the light if you like, I'm going to have a lie down," and the fairy curled up in the top of the rucksack.

Helen looked at Rona's arm. There was a big red weal, about the size of a two-pound coin, on her wrist, and a few smaller ones towards her elbow. But there was no sign of molten plastic sticking to the skin.

"Swimming in the loch must have cleaned your arm. It looks fine but I can put a dressing on if you like."

"No thanks. Not yet. I think I might go for a swim. I'm feeling a bit shaky and I really want to be myself for a while. You don't mind if I leave you with Lavender, do you?"

"No, of course not," said Helen.

Rona leapt from stone to stone down to the waves and was hardly visible by the time she reached the sea, but Helen thought she saw the small grey figure pull on a hooded cloak, then shimmer, shrink and slide into the sea and out of sight.

Helen sat quietly on the beach. She didn't look at her watch, there was no point. It was late, and she would be in trouble when she got home, but there was nothing she could do about it, so she just sat and thought about bears, snakes, newts and bars of iron, and listened to the gentle noise of the waves.

Her thoughts were interrupted by a song, sung without words, with only two or three high sounds, and a strange deep crackling undertone. Helen was sure the simple melody was telling a story; a story of happiness and sadness, questions and surprises, which repeated again and again with no true ending.

The waves, which struck each part of the curved shore at a slightly different time, played a constant soft scraping percussion. The song was coming from the sea, from a rock out by the cliffs to Helen's left. The wind seized the occasional note before it reached her, but she found herself filling in the gaps in her head.

Once she'd heard the melody, she found herself transcribing it in her head for the fiddle. I could play that, she thought, but it would need a proper ending. Then the singing stopped, and only the waves kept playing.

Rona appeared wet and smiling beside Helen five minutes later.

"Was that you singing?" Helen asked.

"Yes. I needed to sing out my feelings about tonight. Lavender's my closest friend and I thought I had brought her here to die. I can't cope without singing and I sing better as a seal. Did you like it?"

"I loved it," Helen grinned. "I'd like to play it but we'd need to write an ending." She looked at Rona.

Rona smiled. "We won't have an ending to our quest song, my human friend, until we have the Book back."

Helen hummed the bars she had imagined for the violin and Rona sang a few other phrases, and soon they had begun to turn a simple melody into a complex harmony. Then all at once Sapphire and Catesby were back, urging the others to leave.

So Helen put the sleeping fairy inside her torn fleece and climbed onto the dragon behind Rona, trying not to touch the very wet sealskin on her back. Just before Sapphire took off, she asked Rona, "Why didn't you become a seal to rescue Lavender from the loch?"

She just caught Rona's answer before the rushing wind deafened her. "I needed a hand to hold her in; as a seal I can only use my teeth ..."

They flew into the night, into the wind, over the sea, back to the place where it all began.

Chapter 11

Helen had found the flight up to Orkney exhilarating but the flight back was exhausting and cold, and she was relieved when Sapphire's wing-beats slowed and the dragon floated to the ground.

They landed just beside the wood where they had left Yann. Helen jumped down and watched the others go into the dark trees, where no moonlight reached.

She lifted Lavender gently out of her fleece, partly to see how she was, and partly to persuade her to make a bit of fairy light, to lift the spooky blackness.

Lavender sneezed and smiled at Helen. "Hello!"

"How do you feel?" Helen asked.

"Fine. Fabulous. A bit damp. This dress is ruined. Oh well. I have plenty of others at home. All ... guess what? ... purple!"

"Don't you like purple?"

"I hate it! Purple dresses, purple slippers, purple ribbons, purple buttons. We all get given flower names, but some fairies get called Tulip or Rose and can wear any colour at all. But I'm *Lavender,* so I can *only* wear purple. My mum is a Bluebell and moans about hating blue, so you'd think she'd have given me a name with more colour variety! But no! She chose Lavender and I'm stuck with purple! It's just not done to go against your name. It's unlucky. And luck is very important to fairies.

"You were my luck tonight though. You saved my life. I will repay you somehow."

Lavender's little balls of light danced round them as they walked into the wood, to join the others under a tall birch tree. Yann was letting Catesby pick small twigs from his hair, while Rona used a handful of dried leaves to wipe white sweat stains from his flank.

"No," he was answering, "I had a really boring night. I just had to gallop to get here to meet you. That's all." He grinned. "So tell me about your adventures."

Rona threw the leaves down and told the tale of the night. Helen listened, slightly embarrassed, as Rona described how the healer's child had saved Lavender's life with magic breath and then pulled the clue from her pocket.

Rona ended her story. "Then we heard the Master bellow as we flew away. He was angry to lose us, but will be even angrier when he fails to find the clue."

Yann walked on soft hooves up to Helen and Lavender. First he held his hand out to Lavender, and she hopped nimbly from Helen to Yann.

"How are you, my smallest fabled friend?"

"I am stiff, and my dress and hair are a mess, but I breathe and I fly." She did a quick somersault on his hand. "I will weave magic for my friends again, because the healer's child saved me."

"How did you save her, healer's child?" Yann turned to Helen. "Is it true you have magic too? Why did you not tell us?"

"It wasn't magic, Yann, I just pressed her chest to restart her heart and blew into her mouth to fill her lungs."

"You did not have time to get that from a book."

"No. My Mum insisted we took a course together on first aid for babies when my wee sister Nicola was born, and I practised artificial resuscitation on a doll. The doll was a bit bigger than Lavender but the principle was the same."

"So you have learnt some healing from your elders after all."

Helen shrugged. "I suppose I have. Mum would be delighted if I could ever tell her. But in fact, she's just going to be massively annoyed when I get home so late. What time is it?"

"It is long past the mid point of night. But it is winter and there are still many hours before dawn. So we have time to puzzle out the next clue."

Helen knew she would be in serious trouble at home for staying out so late, but perhaps a few more minutes wouldn't make the consequences any worse. So she sat on a mossy branch, brought the driftwood from her pocket, and handed it to Yann. Yann read, in his clear hard voice:

"Here there is great change and fear:
Writhing snake to bar of hot iron,
Slippery newt to growling bear.
If you can hold strong and fast,
You will hold me in your hands at last.

"We will hold what in our hands at last? The Book? Is this the last clue?" Yann spoke quietly and thoughtfully. "But where is there great change and fear? You don't get bears on this island any more, nor many blacksmiths with bars of hot iron."

"There were big steelworks many miles west of here until a few years ago," said Helen, "but they've all closed down now. That was a big change, but I think the ground there is too polluted to have snakes or newts, let alone bears."

Yann looked around. "Can anyone puzzle this out for us?"

There was a ripple of shrugs from tired shoulders covered in feathers, scales, damp fur and torn purple fabric.

Helen said, "The bar of iron and the bear do ring a bell with me, perhaps from an old song or story I once heard, but I'm too tired to find it in my head tonight. The Master doesn't have the clue, so we don't have to race him to the next answer. Can't we just sleep on it?"

She stood up and stretched. "I have to go now anyway, because my parents will be worried about me."

She finally looked at her watch. It was 1.30 am. She closed her eyes, then looked again. It was definitely 1.30 am. Her Mum and Dad would be imagining all sorts of terrible things that might have happened to her, though they probably wouldn't get anywhere near the truth.

But she didn't like lying to them. What would she say about her long disappearance? The fabled beasts were all watching her.

"Will you get into trouble, human girl?" asked Yann.

She looked up at him. "Probably. Yes."

"I could help," offered Lavender. "I am in your debt. I could conjure up a forgetting spell, and make your parents forget you have been absent all evening."

"You could brainwash them?" Helen considered the idea. It would be convenient, but she didn't like the idea of anyone messing with her parents' minds. "I don't think so. I think I'll just have to say I'm sorry and nod lots while they shout at me." She sighed.

"Will you tell them where you have been?" asked Yann.

"No. They wouldn't believe me, and I don't want to get you lot into trouble too."

"Will they punish you?" asked Rona.

"Probably. I've never broken this many rules in one go before, so I don't know what will happen. Will your parents be angry with you for staying out so late?"

"Not really. Our parents will not think it is odd. Our peoples are often safer moving around at night. So long as we are ready for the Gathering in two nights' time ..." Rona's voice faltered.

"Which we won't be without the Book," Lavender added, "and then we will be lucky to escape their anger with any of our powers and privileges intact." The fairy sounded all wobbly again, more upset about not getting the Book back than about being attacked by dozens of seagulls.

Then Yann turned suddenly, his head cocked to a sound that Helen hadn't heard, and Rona said, "Shhhh!" to Lavender.

Then they all heard it.

"Hallo! Halloooooo! Helen! Helen Strang!"

A man's voice. Several voices. Coming down the hill towards the clump of trees.

Helen rushed to the edge of the trees and looked out. There was a line of torches, and dark shadows behind the lights. Not just her parents looking for her, but a whole search party looking for a lost child. Well, they could find her, but not her friends.

She ran back into the trees. The shouts were getting louder.

"They're searching for me. I must let them find me before they get any nearer to you. I'll try to work out the clue before tomorrow night. Good luck."

Yann said, "I could get you out of here, before they reach us."

"Thanks, but no. I will sort this out on my own. Don't leave here until all the searchers are gone."

Helen crept back out of the wood, and lay down in a heap in the corner of the nearest field. The line of searchers was still a few minutes away as they were walking very slowly, so she picked up a rock, gritted her teeth and before she could have second thoughts, gave herself a quick dunt on the forehead.

Then she lay still. Waiting to be found.

The shouts got louder and someone scrambled over the fence and stood on Helen's leg. She moaned and he yelled, and suddenly there were people all around, shining torches in her face, and offering her water.

Then the circle of concerned faces cleared and her Mum was there.

"Helen! Darling! Are you alright? Can you talk? What day is it? What's your sister's name? And why aren't you in the garage?"

"Oh, Mum. It's Wednesday night. My sister's called Nicola and I hope she isn't out in the dark too. I just went out for some fresh air. Why are there so many people here?"

"You've been missing for hours! We called out the local hill-walking club to help look for you. Are you hurt?"

Her Mum examined her, finding the bashed head, and lots of other minor injuries that Helen must have got during her night's travels and not even noticed.

Helen felt like a complete fraud. She had been expecting a major row, which she thoroughly deserved, but instead she was carried down the hill by Mr Brydon's eldest son, and given hot chocolate and caramel wafers in the kitchen. Her Mum put plasters and creams on her grazes and bruises, and her Dad poured hot toddies for all the hill-walking club.

Finally everyone left, and Helen was allowed to climb slowly up the stairs with her Mum.

"A few days in bed, and then we'll see if you're fit to be up and about again, my dear."

"I'll be fine tomorrow, really."

The bashed head had seemed like a good way of explaining her disappearance, but she had to get to school tomorrow to look through Mr Crombie's old books of ballads and traditional tales, where she was sure she would find an iron bar and a growling bear.

"I feel much better already. Just give me lots more chocolate for breakfast and I'll be raring to go."

Her Mum helped Helen out of her clothes and into her pyjamas then sat on the edge of the bed waiting for her to fall asleep.

"I know I'm grumpy at you sometimes," she whispered when Helen's breathing slowed, "but I love you very much."

"I know," Helen replied under her breath.

As soon as her Mum left, she sat up with a start. Where was the first aid kit? Thank goodness she hadn't still been wearing it when the searchers found her, but had she left it in the trees or on the rocky beach?

She just hoped she wouldn't need it again.

Chapter 12

The voice boomed, *"Get me that clue!"*

"The centaur colt has it. He is safe in the midst of the centaur tribe. None of your creatures, not even I, Master, can get past their sight and strength and great sharp hooves. While he stays with his father, he is safe and the clue is out of our reach. But, while he stays there, he cannot find the Book."

"You are failing me, Frass. You are letting me down. You do *not* want to disappoint me."

"No, Master. Never. But we can rest today and then follow each of them tonight. We know their lairs and can follow them as they search."

"I am not a follower! I am a leader! I do not wish to get all these clues second hand. I wish to be there first. To let *them* walk into *my* trap. Find out where they are

going. Find out before the sun goes down, Frass, or I will make a flywhisk with your stinking hairy little tail."

"Winter days are very short, Master. Perhaps a little more time ...?"

"No more time!"

Helen woke up feeling like she really did need a day off school. Her head hurt where she'd hit it, she had bruises on both knees from tripping over the clue at the stone circle, her hands were grazed from the struggle with the rough fishing net, and her back was stiff from sitting on Sapphire for so long.

She pulled the duvet over her head and tried to go back to sleep. But she couldn't. She had a perfect excuse for a couple of days off school, but she wasn't able to take advantage of it.

She knew the answer to the riddle was in the school. The more she thought about the song she half-remembered, the more she was sure she'd heard an older girl sing it, years ago, at one of Mr Crombie's traditional Scottish ceilidh nights.

Then, she remembered that her excuse for leaving the house yesterday had been to think about a solo. If she didn't have one by tonight's rehearsal, then Mr Crombie might phone the summer school director and tell her not to bother coming.

But she had nothing to play. No one would be impressed if she just trudged her way through a hornpipe or a waltz. Suddenly, Helen grinned, and rolled out from under the warm duvet. She grabbed her violin off her desk and tightened her bow.

She warmed up with a few Christmas carols and scales. Then, once her fingers had woken up, Helen played the tune she had realized was going to be her solo. At first, she played it slowly, carefully, hoping it would sound the same on the violin as it did in her head. Then she played it faster, louder, more confidently, over and over again, until she was sure it was perfect.

She bounced down the stairs to breakfast and marched into the kitchen all smiles, ready to show everyone how fit and well she was.

"Goodness me, Helen, you look *dreadful*," said her Dad.

"I feel fine. Just a bit bruised." Helen pulled up her pyjama trouser legs and showed her bashed knees. "Really, I'm fine. I can go to school."

Her Mum looked in her eyes with a professional frown. "Not after a bang on the head and prolonged unconsciousness, Helen. I want to keep you with me today."

"The school is only down the road, Mum, and they have your mobile number."

"Why on earth are you so keen to go to school?"

"The school concert's next week, and there's a rehearsal tonight," Helen explained. "I have to play my solo for Mr Crombie tonight, or he'll tell the director of the summer school not to bother coming to hear me."

"Oh yes ... the summer school." Her Mum sat down beside Helen, still looking concerned. "I know music is your favourite hobby, but it does seem to be taking up an awful lot of your time. Especially if a whole evening's rehearsing means you need fresh air so much that you wander up a hill in the dark. Perhaps you should give yourself a break from music for a while?"

Dad put his hand on Helen's shoulder, to stop her answering too forcefully.

"Music is good for her brain as well as her soul, Tricia."

"I suppose so, but this summer school is for very serious musicians, and even Mr Crombie isn't sure you're preparing seriously enough, is he? And he's usually your biggest fan."

"Nonsense," said Dad, ruffling Helen's hair, "I'm Helen's biggest fan," and he gave her a big hug and a bowl of chocolate cereal.

But Helen was determined not to be diverted from her campaign to get to the library. She sat down beside her Mum. "I really must go to school, play my solo to Mr Crombie and do some research in the library. If I feel sick, or get stars in front of my eyes, or anything, I'll let the school office know and they can call you ... or they can even call a real *people* doctor."

That got a smile from her Mum. "Don't be cheeky! Alright, you can go to school and your precious rehearsal, but then you will have a very early night. Agreed?"

Helen thought that was extremely unlikely, but she smiled at her Mum anyway. She hadn't managed more than a mouthful of her cereal when there was a high pitched squeal from upstairs and a series of panicked giggles.

Helen's Mum yelled from her place at the table, "Come down for your breakfast, Nicola, and stop making such a racket."

But Nicola kept calling, "Mummy, Mummy come."

Her Mum sighed, got up from the table and headed out of the door, just as Nicola shouted in her clear little voice, "Mummy, look. A fairy. A burple fairy. In Hen's room."

Helen dropped her spoon and ran for the door. She sprinted up the stairs after her Mum. Nicola was almost singing now, from the doorway to Helen's room.

"Fairy! Fairy! Fairy fairy fairy!"

Helen tried to overtake on the landing but her Mum lengthened her stride and put her hand on Nicola's head.

"Fairies? Really? That's nice. Come and have some toast." Helen squeezed past them into her room and looked round frantically. She couldn't see any fairies.

"Come and see!" insisted Nicola. "Come and see! A fairy, Mummy!"

"There's no such thing as fairies, darling, except in books and pantomimes. Come and have some toast."

Nicola burst into tears, and threw her bright pink teddy at her Mum.

"Is so a fairy! Is so a fairy!"

Mum was about to get very annoyed about the bear knocking her glasses squint, when Helen knelt down by her sister and looked into Nicola's little wet face. "Would you like to show *me* the fairy? Seeing as this is my room."

"You don't have to interrupt your breakfast, Helen, love. She was seeing mermaids in the bath last night."

"No, it's okay. It'll make her happy, then we can all have breakfast." So Helen's Mum stomped off back down the stairs and Helen picked her sister up.

"Where was the fairy?"

Nicola pointed up to the ceiling and whirled her hand round. "Whizzing."

"Whizzing up there? And what did she look like?"

"Burple and pretty."

"I think she's gone now but thank you for telling me. You can tell me any time you see fairies, and I'll always believe you."

With a happy little girl in her arms, she went back downstairs, and heard her Mum in the kitchen, saying: "Where do they get it from, all this nonsense? I thought I was bringing up children with a rational scientific attitude to the world, and what do we get? Fairies and fiddle music."

Helen searched her room for Lavender after breakfast, calling her name softly, but found no sign of the fairy. She hoped Nicola had just imagined a 'burple fairy,' and that there was no ominous message or sudden emergency awaiting her.

So she left for school, looking as healthy and cheerful as possible, and trying hard not to limp. About quarter of a mile from the school she met up with Kirsty, who was desperate to talk about the night's excitement.

"My Dad was out hunting for you. He says you could have died of hypothermia if you'd stayed out all night. I don't think he'll even let me take the rubbish out after dark now. What on earth happened?"

So Helen had to tell more lies. She really wanted to tell her best friend that selkies could sing and that fairies had very limited wardrobes, but instead she had to tell her the same nonsense about falling and banging her head. She had to repeat the story several times in the playground too. It was a relief when the school bell went.

The morning dragged, as they drew diagrams of the earth tilting round the sun to show why the days were shortest and the nights longest at the winter solstice. When the lunch bell rang, Helen grabbed her schoolbag and ran to the old school building.

As soon as she reached the library, she delved in her bag for the copy of the clue she'd scribbled down in her notebook. Her hand touched something warm and wriggling!

She dropped the school bag and fell backwards, imagining which of the Master's creatures could be in her bag, waiting to sink its fangs into her. As she crashed into a set of shelves and sat down hard on the floor, a little voice said, "Please get me out of here, I've got my wings tangled in a mitten."

Helen picked up her bag gently and looked inside. It was Lavender!

"What on earth are you doing in there?" Helen scooped Lavender out of the bottom of her schoolbag.

"I hid in here from your very sweet little baby human and then I fell asleep. I woke up when you were in a room with a woman who sounded like my Aunt Poppy explaining the ancient laws of magical combat, so I stayed quiet until you were alone."

"I was about to search for books that might help us with the clue. Do you want to help?"

Lavender was staring at the ceiling-high shelves of books. "What is this place? Is it a book graveyard?"

"It's the school library. We keep books here that all the classes need, like atlases and dictionaries, as well as lots of old books that no one reads but no one wants to throw out. I probably need to look through those."

"I've only ever seen the Book itself and the book you have in your green bag. I didn't know there were so many books in the world. Do these have all the answers too?

"Not really. Most books only deal with very small bits of the world. If you want answers to everything, you need to use a computer. But with computers you need to know exactly the right question, and you can't always trust the answer."

"You can always trust our Book." Lavender flew up to the top shelf and gently touched the spines of the dusty books. "Are there other places like this?"

"Oh yes. Universities have libraries hundreds of times this size, and there are bookshops so big they have cafés in them. Let's start looking for Mr Crombie's books of ballads."

"No!" said Lavender, floating back down, "I must do something first.

"I must repay my debt to you. My aunts say you must always repay debts quickly, before they fester. I like being your friend, so I don't want this to stay between us.

"You didn't want my forgetting spell yesterday, and Yann says you don't want a vision of your future husband, so I have another idea."

Lavender perched on top of a bin for recycling paper, reached her left hand over her right shoulder, and, scrunching up her face, pulled out a shiny purple feather from her wing.

"Here." She held it out to Helen.

"Don't you need it?"

"I will grow another one eventually, but I want you to have it and keep it with you always. The feather is still part of me, so I will always be able to find it. If you are ever lost, or in danger, I will be able to find you, as long as you keep the feather with you. This is a promise that I will save your life if I can. And that promise repays my debt."

Lavender held the feather out again.

Helen took it solemnly between her thumb and finger. "I will keep it and treasure it. And now that I have it, you don't owe me anything at all. We're friends because we like each other."

She threaded the feather into the strap of her watch and smiled at Lavender.

"Right. Let's look for change and fear and bears and bars of iron."

While Helen knelt down to check the lower shelves, Lavender flew back up to the top ones.

"Having a fairy in the library certainly saves shifting the wheelie ladder around." Helen tilted her head sideways to read the spines of the books on the bottom shelf.

"What are all these stone heads?" Lavender asked as she skipped along the highest shelf.

"Those are busts, statues of famous people's heads and shoulders. They're the former headmasters of the school, local poets and people like that. Don't bump into them. I don't want one to fall on my head."

"They're all men!" exclaimed Lavender.

"Yes. By the time women started running schools and

writing poetry, people had stopped carving heads and had started taking photos."

It was fun having Lavender with her, but the fairy did keep asking questions.

"What are the carvings on the ceiling?"

"Coats of arms, stuff about battles. No bears or bars of iron. Keep looking for books of ballads or old Scottish stories, Lavender."

"Can you smell something? Something a bit pongy?"

"No, Lavender, I can't. People bring the weirdest things for packed lunches. Keep going along the shelves, please."

"Helen, it is common to have fairies on people's ...?" but Helen interrupted her before she could finish the question.

"I've found it! Lavender! Listen to this ... A boy called Tam Linn was stolen by the fairies ... bigger fairies than you, I think ... and became the favourite knight of the fairy queen. He was the guardian of a wood for the fairy queen, and there he met a girl called Janet and they fell in love ... ho hum ... and she rescued him from his enchantment by holding fast to him when the fairy queen turned him into all sorts of scary things like ... bars of hot iron and serpents! Then the queen went off in a huff and Tam Linn became mortal again. And Tam Linn married Janet and they lived happily ever et cetera et cetera.

"That sounds right doesn't it?"

"Absolutely! You are so clever with these books! And the holding fast, that's what we have to do when we find the Book or a clue!"

"And the best bit is ..." Helen flicked a few pages back

in the book, "The best bit is that this isn't some fairy tale like Cinderella that could come from any country. This one's set in Scotland, in the Borders. The song and the stories mention the wood by name. Carterhaugh Woods by Ettrick Water, near Selkirk. That's just a few miles from here."

She turned to Lavender, "Do your family live near there? Are the fairies in this story your people?"

"Oh no. If Tam Linn's fairy folk were forest dwellers and took human children, then they weren't flower fairies like me. Fairy stories are very imprecise. You call my people fairies, and you have fairy godmothers and fairy folk in the forest. But we are all different. The forest folk would eat flower fairies like me in one mouthful, if they could catch us, which isn't easy as they don't have wings. But there aren't any of them in these parts now, as far as I know. There is hardly enough true forest left for them."

Lavender sniffed. "There's that smell again. Do books smell bad in big groups?"

"Not usually. Never mind. We can go now, we've got the answer. Do you want to go in my bag again?"

"Not really. It has lots of pointy things in it. I must get home now. My Aunt Lily needs me to make long-lasting lights for the Gathering."

"Can you let Rona and the rest know the answer to the riddle right now?"

Lavender shook her head. "I don't think so. We don't all live in the same place, so we had planned to meet tonight in the wood. If you can come, we can all go to Carterhaugh. If not, I'll tell them the answer and we will go without you."

"I'll try to be there, if I can stop my parents fussing over me."

Lavender hugged Helen and flew through a broken pane of glass in a window that overlooked the overgrown school garden.

Helen left the library and went to eat her packed lunch very quickly in the canteen, where fortunately no one seemed to be eating weird, pongy food.

Chapter 13

Mr Crombie raised his eyebrows hopefully at Helen as she walked into the chilly hall for the concert rehearsal that afternoon.

She grinned at him. "When would you like me to play the solo I've been working on? Before the Christmas music or after?"

"We'll warm up with the carols first, then hear what you've come up with," he replied smiling.

So the band scraped and clattered their way through O' Little Town of Bethlehem and the other carols they were starting to get bored with, before – finally – it was Helen's turn.

She took a few steps in front of the rest of the children and played directly to Mr Crombie.

She played the tune that Rona had sung off the

stone beach on Orkney the night before, which she and Rona had developed and strengthened together. The music that told of the loss of the Book, the quest to find it, as well as the fears and frustrations of their failures.

She played it twice, once in a major key and once in a minor key. Then she lifted her chin from the fiddle and waited, wondering how the quest song had sounded to an audience who weren't searching for answers or fearful of monsters. Would it mean anything to them?

Everyone was silent for a moment.

"Where did you find that?" Mr Crombie asked.

"A friend and I wrote it."

"You wrote it?"

"Parts of it. It's not completely finished, but I'll know how it ends long before Monday."

"It is very, very good, Helen," Mr Crombie beamed at her. "A strong and mature piece of music. It will definitely be worth the director's time coming to hear you play that. You have produced something totally original and extremely beautiful. Does it have a title?"

"I thought maybe I'd call it *Solstice.*"

"Lovely. Well, you obviously don't need to rehearse it any more with us. I'm sure I can rely on you to find an ending by Monday, and as we'd all love to hear that ending please try not to lose yourself on our hillsides again between now and Christmas Eve."

Kirsty grabbed Helen's arm as she was carefully packing her fiddle away.

"So, who's the friend that wrote the music with you, then?"

"I can't … I can't really say."

"Why not? I know I'm not as good a violinist as you, but we did used to play together when we were first learning. Have you found some fancier friends now? Some other musical geniuses? Is that why you want to go to this summer school?"

"No! This friend is different."

"Different how, exactly?"

Helen considered her answer. "It's just someone I've been chatting with recently at nights. You know, a bit like an online chat room."

"About music?"

"Music and books and stuff."

"Not someone at a different school? Not someone that you'll be pally with once we go to the High School?"

Helen laughed. "Definitely not someone I'll be pally with at the High School. You're still my best friend, Kirsty. But just like you don't bother to talk to me about football, I'm allowed to have friends to talk to about music and … you know … other stuff."

"I suppose so. Can you come to mine for tea then? Rather than chat to your cyber mates."

"Sorry. Mum wants me home and in bed like a good little invalid. Soon though. Very soon. After the solstice I'm bound to have more time."

"After the solstice? After the concert you mean."

"Yeah. That's what I meant."

Helen walked slowly out of the school hall and stood for a while in the shadow of the buildings. She should have been delighted; Mr Crombie was impressed with her solo, and she was confident that if she could come up with an ending, then the summer school director would be impressed too.

But she had lied to Kirsty again, and was about to lie to her Mum once more, which didn't seem right when she was searching for a Book about questions, answers and truth. Also her life seemed to be split down the middle into day and night, and she wasn't getting enough sleep in either half.

It was nearly dark already, as the weak winter sun was covered by thick grey clouds. She wouldn't even have time for a nap before night fell. She started to walk slowly towards the school gates, when she realized that her Mum's Landrover was waiting in the car park.

"I thought you would like a lift home. Rest your bruised legs."

"Thanks, but don't you have surgery just now?"

"No, I cancelled it. I wanted to be sure you were okay."

"I'd like a nice big tea and an early night actually."

That definitely wasn't a lie. She wasn't going to get to sleep, but she did desperately want to.

"I've made lentil soup and fresh bread. We'll eat that, then you can have a bath and get to bed. How was the rehearsal?"

"Great. Mr Crombie likes my solo."

"Really? Super. I can't wait to hear it. When's the concert?"

"Monday. Dad's written it on the kitchen calendar."

"We'll definitely be there then!"

Helen ate like a soldier about to march to war, then just as the sun was sliding from behind the clouds to behind the hills, she clambered into bed, watched carefully by her Mum.

As soon as her Mum was out of the room, Helen got up and dressed as warmly as possible. Then she opened her bedroom window and looked down.

This was the only way out of the house without being heard. Her Dad was reading Nicola a bedtime story in the living room, while her Mum was hanging washing on the pulley in the kitchen. There was no way out downstairs. She would *have* to leave by the window. And she didn't have time to make a rope out of sheets, or a parachute from a duvet cover.

Helen's bedroom was above the front door, which was protected from the Scottish weather by a little stone porch.

Whenever Helen had daydreamed about leaving the house unseen on a secret mission, she had always thought this porch would be a handy way out.

Now, she squeezed out of her open window, sat on the sill and pulled the window almost shut behind her. She turned round and lowered herself slowly backwards until she was holding onto the sill by her fingers. Her toes just reached the sloping stone below her. She let go and dropped to a crouch on the porch roof.

Now she was no higher off the ground than Nicola at the top of the climbing frame. She grasped the edge of the porch and swung herself down.

The drop was a little further than it looked. Helen didn't breathe for a minute after landing on the hard path, partly because she couldn't and partly because she was listening for any reaction indoors. But no one came rushing out, so she hoped no one had heard her thump down.

She stood up and waggled her legs. Everything still seemed to work, and she didn't have any more bruises than when she had got out of bed. So she jogged up the hill, feeling underdressed without her green rucksack.

It was fully dark by the time she reached the woods, but she followed a glow of fairy light. The friends were just settling down, Sapphire heating the air with her glowing open mouth and Rona handing round some small brown cakes.

Helen took one, and nibbled it. It was a bit like a salty scone.

"Seaweed cakes," Rona said, "to give us all strength."

Then Yann announced, "I have solved the riddle."

"So have I," responded Helen.

There was a moment of silence. Then Helen smiled, "You first. Lavender knows what I found, so I'm not going to copy you if your answer is better."

"There can be only one answer, human child."

"True. I know what it is. And it's not far from here. On you go."

Yann humphed, and put on his best declaiming voice.

"The riddle refers to an old tale about a human who was privileged to join the fairy queen's band, but was forced to return to human life by a local girl. The man was called Tam Linn, and the story ends in a battle at Tam Linn's Well in Carterhaugh Woods, where he tried to escape the human girl's clutches by turning into various loathly animals and a hot bar of iron. But the girl held fast and he could not escape and he lost the fairy queen for ever.

"So we must go to Carterhaugh. Do you agree, healer's child?"

"I agree that we must go to Carterhaugh, but you've told the story all wrong," Helen said indignantly. "Janet saved Tam Linn. He asked her to show courage and hold fast however the fairy queen changed him. He wanted to become human again and escape from the fairy queen."

"Why would anyone wish to be human – boringly, prosaically human – when they could live a life of stories, songs and magic with the forest folk? Janet was jealous of him and the fairy queen, and couldn't let go of him, even though Tam Linn wanted her to."

"Nonsense! He was stolen away by the fairies, as children have always been, and was very lucky to meet a woman strong and brave enough to save him."

Rona broke in, "Hold on! You may not agree on the story, but you do agree on the answer to the riddle! You have both heard different versions of the story, of course you have. Helen has heard the one Tam Linn and Janet told their children, and Yann has heard the version the fairy folk told. And they are both true to themselves."

"If mine is the version Tam Linn told, it must be the truth," Helen muttered.

"Helen!" scolded Rona. "You two can argue about this anytime you like once we have the Book."

"Once we have the Book, we'll not need her anymore," snorted Yann.

"We all need friends, Yann," said Rona. "Now how do we get to Carterhaugh and can we get going right now?"

Sapphire and Catesby suddenly got quite animated.

Rona explained that both flying beasts used the various rivers running into the River Tweed —like the Ettrick Water, Gala Water, Jed Water and the Teviot — to navigate around the nearby hills. They could easily find Carterhaugh by using the rivers, even with clouds covering the stars and moon.

Catesby immediately started drawing an incredibly detailed map on the ground that showed the sources and courses of all the rivers in the Borders. Sapphire watched for a moment, then snorted and wiped the bird's thin scratched lines away with one sweep of her claws. Drawing a deep line in the ground, she showed the way from Helen's village of Clovenshaws to Ettrick Water near Selkirk, then a simple map showing Tam Linn's Well in a small patch of grass between a strip of woods and a narrow track, just one field's length from the river. Catesby shrugged his wings.

It was decided that Catesby would guide Yann, and Sapphire would carry the rest. The dragon's party would get there a little faster and could lie low near the river to check that no one else was there, so they could go straight to the well when Yann and the phoenix arrived.

Yann left immediately, but Helen delayed before getting on the dragon's back. "Did I leave the first aid kit here last night, when I rushed out to stop the search?"

Lavender threw out a few brighter light balls and they all had a quick look. Helen found the battered green bag by the tree stump she usually sat on.

She waved it at the others. "Found it. Let's hope we don't need it!"

Rona said, "Yann was wrong. We don't *just* need you to help us find the Book. We do need you now because you have a knowledge of books that we can't match but, when we find the Book, we *will* still want to meet up with you to chat, play music and take you on adventures."

"Yann won't," Helen sighed.

"Yann has spent all day with his father, and that makes him very grumpy."

Helen humphed, making Lavender laugh. "You sound just like Yann! He always makes horsey, snorting noises when he's grumpy!"

"I'm not grumpy. I think I might be scared. Do you think the Master is there waiting for us?"

Rona reassured her. "He didn't get the stone circle clue before us, did he? So they don't know where we are going. Even if they have followed us here, they won't get to Carterhaugh before we do. None of his creatures can move as fast as a healthy dragon can fly. I think this time we are ahead of him."

And so the friends flew off in a wide curve, to confuse any watchers on the ground, and headed for Tam Linn's Well.

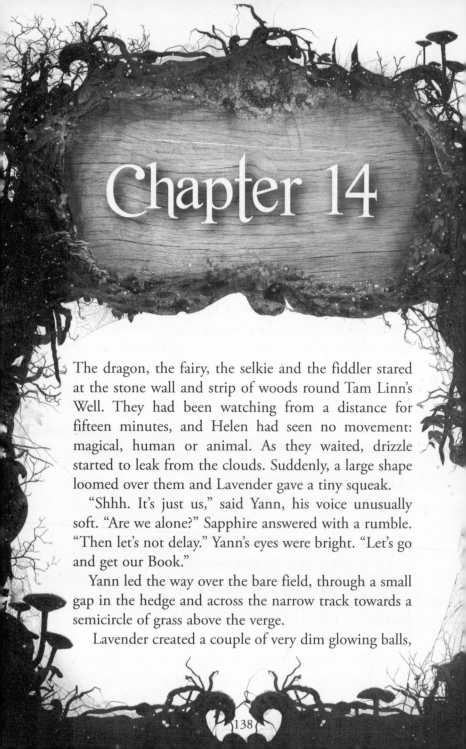

Chapter 14

The dragon, the fairy, the selkie and the fiddler stared at the stone wall and strip of woods round Tam Linn's Well. They had been watching from a distance for fifteen minutes, and Helen had seen no movement: magical, human or animal. As they waited, drizzle started to leak from the clouds. Suddenly, a large shape loomed over them and Lavender gave a tiny squeak.

"Shhh. It's just us," said Yann, his voice unusually soft. "Are we alone?" Sapphire answered with a rumble. "Then let's not delay." Yann's eyes were bright. "Let's go and get our Book."

Yann led the way over the bare field, through a small gap in the hedge and across the narrow track towards a semicircle of grass above the verge.

Lavender created a couple of very dim glowing balls,

giving little light and throwing lots of complicated shadows.

Helen could see a rectangular stone trough against a curved wall. Water dripped into it from a stone spout above. All the stonework was covered with damp dark moss. She looked above and around her, constantly checking for movement. There was a hill rising beyond the wall, covered in old trees and bushes; all that was left of the fairy queen's forest. One huge tree overhung the well; although bare of leaves for winter, its trunk was shiny with ivy.

Everything was still.

They were too far now from Ettrick Water to hear its splash and flow. There were no cars, no birds. Only the light tapping of the drizzle on grass and trees.

Rona strode straight to the well and stuck her hand in. She methodically searched the bottom of the trough. "Nothing here."

"Try the spout." Helen and Yann spoke at exactly the same time. Helen turned to Yann and smiled nervously. He grinned back.

Rona's slim fingers investigated the ridge in the stone spout sticking out from the wall.

"Yes!"

She pulled out a small, dripping package and carried it over to the others. As they stood in the centre of the grassy space, under the branches of the tree, her shining wet fingers unfolded a large, irregularly-shaped piece of leather. They all reached out to touch it, then Yann said, "We must hold it fast, like Janet."

So they grasped the ragged edges of the leather with their right hands or claws. Helen had just opened her mouth to say, "Now let's read it," when there was a sudden sound from above them. A hiss.

They looked up at the silhouettes of branches and twigs against the dark grey sky. The branches were moving; not blowing in the wind, but shifting and slithering.

"Hold on!" yelled Yann as shapes and hisses dropped heavily from the tree onto them and the leather they all held.

At first, Helen thought the tree had fallen on them, but the branches were coiling and writhing tightly round her forehead and wrists. She realized with horror that she was covered in snakes.

They all cried out at once, screams and moans and shouts of fear. But only Yann used words.

"Hold fast!" he yelled again.

Helen felt a snake creep right round her neck, hissing into her ear, and she used her left hand to haul the snake off and throw it into the well. Her throat was free again but she was having difficulty breathing, as the feeling of snakes slithering round her body had brought her to the edge of panic.

"Don't let go!" ordered Yann. "The Book says we have to hold fast."

"We should run fast, not hold fast," gasped Helen. She knocked a snake off Rona's head and kicked away another that was trying to climb up her own leg.

They were all trying to escape the snakes without letting go of the clue. They were standing on each other's feet, tripping over snakes and slipping on the wet grass. Then Helen smelt a smell; a farmy smell, a goaty smell. She suddenly realized it was the smell that she had dismissed at lunchtime when Lavender had kept nagging her about it.

"Oh no! They were with us in the library! They heard us when we found the clue!"

"Yes, you were very helpful, human girl. You know our silly little stories better than we know them ourselves."

She twisted round, to see where the sniggering voice was coming from.

"Now, children. Give me the clue."

They were surrounded by dark shapes, almost as tall as men but with flicking tails behind them, and what seemed to be great hairy trousers.

"Fauns!" snorted Yann. "Always the Master's little helpers. I'm not afraid of you, you stinking two-legged creatures."

"You should be, colt. You should be terrified of us," growled the largest of the fauns. "Now give me the clue."

Yann said simply, "No."

"Give me the clue, or you will regret it."

Yann repeated quietly, "No."

Then Helen whispered, "No," and the others said it too. "No. No. No." None of them would be the first to let go.

"One last chance, children. Give me that clue!"

This time they all answered in one strong voice. "NO!"

The fauns leapt on them. Using their strong men's arms, and their powerful goat legs, they tried to pull the children away and grasp the leather themselves. But the circle of friends stayed close and held on tight.

Helen gritted her teeth against the smell, the whipping of tails, the grabbing of hands and the snakes still coiling round her.

The circle round the clue didn't let go. They couldn't really fight, as they had their backs to their attackers, or at best could only turn side on, but they could use their free arms, claws or wings to defend the friend standing at their side, and they could all stamp on snakes and kick goaty legs.

For a moment or two, in a strangely quiet battle, the friends held firm. There was hissing, breathing and grunting. But no more words.

When Helen felt her grip on the wet leather slipping, she dug her nails in, made a fist and crumpled up her edge of the clue as tight as she could. She had tears running down her face and hardly knew what she was doing, but any time she saw a snake on Rona to her left she threw it off, and knew that Yann was doing the same for her to her right. Whenever she felt a faun behind her, she kicked back into its legs or thrust an elbow into its belly.

But how long could they hold on? What use was holding fast when they needed to escape?

Then she felt movement under her feet. Thinking it was another snake, she stamped her heel down, but her heel sank into crumbling soil. The ground was shifting; rising in a dome shape under their feet.

There was a sudden explosion of earth and turf. A massive black shape rose out of the ground, bellowing and shaking a great heavy head free of earth. As the creature reared up, two huge curved horns pierced the leather and pulled the clue up and away from the circle of friends. They held fast for as long as they could, but as they were lifted off the ground, their own weight ripped the clue from their grasp.

Then the snakes and fauns fell on them from all sides.

Helen still had her hand in a fist but the leather had slipped away. She used the fist to hit the nearest faun, then looked around her.

Lavender had held on longest to the leather, fluttering on the edge, but she was thrown off as the huge monster shook his head and the leather flapped violently. Helen caught Lavender as the fairy fell backwards through the air, then she tried to run for the river but tripped over a snake at her feet. She fell onto the wet grass and curled up round Lavender, surrounded by a chaos of stamping and trampling.

Helen raised herself onto her hands and knees and tried to crawl away but, as soon as she moved, sharp hooves kicked into her ribs and legs. She sank down again, and the kicking stopped. All she could do was make her body into a barrier between those hooves and her smallest and most fragile friend.

Even with her eyes closed, Helen could still see the monster. A huge hairy black head with twisted silver horns, resting on massive shoulders. An animal's head and a man's shoulders. The Master of the Maze; a Minotaur with a bull's head and a man's body.

But his head was not like the bulls her mother treated. It was not the head of a farm animal, but of an ancient creature; a huge, violent, prehistoric steer or aurochs.

Helen became aware of fewer thuds on the grass round her head. Perhaps the fauns had moved away? Perhaps she could escape now? She lifted her head slowly to find a snake's beady eyes only a tongue flick from her face.

She shivered and slid one hand out from under her to grab the snake. An air-crushing roar erupted from the well. The snake lowered its head and slithered off. Helen twisted round to see what was happening behind her.

Sapphire was crouched on the ground, hissing and rumbling, but not attacking the fauns. The largest faun stood in front of the dragon, holding Rona and taunting, "If you light a fire, lizard breath, I will grill seal meat on it."

Catesby flew at a faun's face, but the faun ducked, grabbed the phoenix's left wing, swung him round and let go. The bird crashed into the tree trunk and fell in a heap at the base of the wall.

Yann was struggling with two fauns, who were clinging to his horse's back and grabbing him round the neck. He reared up, threw them off, then pivoted round and kicked at the huge shape of the Minotaur.

The clue was no longer on the creature's horns but held in his human hands, rolled up like an old parchment.

The Master held the roll high in triumph and laughed at Yann. Then he shouted in a hoarse strangled voice, "The clue is mine! The Book is mine! The answers will all be mine!"

"Never!" screamed Yann, and lashed out again, catching the Master on the side of the head with one of his heavy front hooves.

The Minotaur stepped beneath the flying front hooves, hooked one massive foot round Yann's back hooves while the centaur was still off balance, and lifted the horse's belly on to his man's shoulder. Using Yann's own weight and momentum to flip him into the air like a toy, the Master sent him crashing to the ground.

Yann looked small and crumpled on the grass as the Master towered over him.

There was silence. Every one of the friends was unmoving on the ground or held in the strong arms of a faun.

"What shall we do with them, my victorious Master?" asked the largest faun.

"Leave them to lick their wounds and savour their failure, Frass," the Master's voice grated. "When I have the power of the Book, these children will be the first to bow down before me, in front of their proud parents."

The Master turned and stepped off the grass. His bare feet booming on the road, he walked away from Tam Linn's well. The snakes vanished into the trees and the fauns trotted after their master.

Lavender was crying in Helen's quivering arms. Catesby was squawking feebly at the base of the stone wall. Rona and Sapphire were hugging, both sobbing. And Yann was lying, motionless, on the ground.

Chapter 15

Helen was shivering. She stood up slowly. "Who's hurt?"
No one answered.

"Who's hurt?" she asked again.

"We're all hurt," gasped Rona. "But what we have done can never be fixed."

"We'll worry about the clue and the Book once we're all warm and moving. Who's hurt the most?" insisted Helen. "Everyone stand up, try to walk or fly. Tell me if anything's broken or bleeding, or if you're faint or light-headed."

"I can move," whispered Lavender.

"Me too," said Rona. Sapphire grunted.

Catesby squawked weakly. Rona crawled over to the wall and picked up a heap of dull brown feathers. "Catesby can't move his right wing," she called.

Helen said, "Keep him still. I'll look at him in a minute." Then she walked stiffly over to Yann.

"Yann. Can you move? Yann. Can you hear me?" There was no movement, no sound. "Yann, please. Oh please, Yann!"

She knelt down by his head and looked into his face. His eyes were closed. "Lavender, more light here, please."

Yann turned his head away from her, away from Lavender's light.

"Oh thank goodness," whispered Helen.

"Go away. Just go away and leave me alone. I don't want to be healed. I'd rather be dead than bow down before that creature."

"Yann, he's not won yet. He's only got the clue, not the Book. Don't give up. Tell me what hurts."

Yann scrambled to his hooves, and yelled in Helen's face.

"I'll tell you what hurts! We were set a test by the Book *and we failed.* We just had to hold fast; just hold fast like some mere human girl managed many years ago ... and we failed. We have all this power, knowledge, strength and magic but we lacked the courage to hold on. We failed and we don't deserve the Book."

Helen looked at him and said briskly, "Well, you can move and you aren't bleeding too much. I diagnose damaged pride. Catesby however has a *real* damaged wing, so I'm going to fix that first."

She turned her back on Yann, and limped over to the phoenix. His right wing was crooked, and his head was lolling on Rona's hand.

Helen said, "I need lots of light, Lavender, and Yann, could you come and open the first aid kit for me?"

147

Yann humphed, but took the green rucksack from Helen. She asked for her exotic animals book, and leafed through it to the section on parrots and birds of paradise. Light rain fell on the pages, but she wiped the words dry and read the short paragraph on broken wings:

"Exotic birds with broken wings, like race horses with broken legs, are usually permanently damaged. It is advisable to put them out of their misery rather than waste resources repairing them."

Helen looked at Catesby, then glanced at Yann. She shook her head and mumbled, "Well, that just won't do."

Then she tried to feel the bird's wing, but as soon as she touched it, he stiffened and squawked in pain.

She asked Yann for the syringe of painkiller and read the sticker on the box that listed how many millilitres was recommended for each size of animal. She estimated that Catesby weighed about the same as a cockerel, and gave him a little less than the stated amount just to be safe. As soon as Helen injected the drug he relaxed in Rona's hands, and she was able to feel that the wing was broken halfway between the shoulder and elbow joints. It seemed to be a simple fracture, broken in only one place.

"Can you find a splint in the bag?" she asked Yann.

"I think the fauns must have kicked you a couple of times," he said. "The splints are in pieces."

"They kicked me more than a couple of times," she replied, "but I need a splint before we can move Catesby. Lavender and Sapphire, can you hunt for a thin branch about the length of my forearm and as straight as possible?"

Lavender found a branch, and Sapphire brought it

carefully to Helen, who used sticky tape to bind it gently to the wing.

"I'll need to take Catesby home and do this properly with a real splint and tape that isn't damp, otherwise his wing will heal squint and he won't be able to fly."

Catesby squawked quietly and Helen raised her eyebrows at Rona.

"Phoenixes heal fast," Rona explained, "so if you can help him keep his wing straight, he will soon be able to fly again. He thanks you for taking away the pain. If you hadn't done that he may have had to burn himself up, and then he wouldn't have hatched again in time to help us find the Book."

"So, phoenixes really do burn and become eggs again?"

"Oh yes, but they can only do it seven times, so they don't like to waste it."

Helen took off her fleece and wrapped the bird in it. Yann shoved everything back in the rucksack and handed it to her.

"Thank you for helping me," she said.

"I was helping Catesby," he replied and turned away.

Helen rummaged in the front pocket of the rucksack, where her Mum kept a human first aid kit. Underneath the plasters were some Arnica tablets, which she insisted that everyone suck, to stop their bashes and bumps becoming bruises.

Yann raised his voice and got everyone's attention.

"We must find the Master, before he finds the Book, but how?"

Lavender answered, "I saw a little of the clue when I was holding it. I saw the words 'brothers and sisters.' Does that help?"

"That's not enough to get to the Book before him. Any other ideas?"

Rona said, "The clue was badly ripped when his horns tore it from our grasp. I think he will have to repair it before he can read it. If we can find his lair before he reads the clue, we might be able to work it out before he can."

It was decided that Helen would take Catesby home and splint his wing, while the others would split up and ask questions of their elders and their storytellers; those who might know where the Minotaur lurked when he was in Scotland.

"But don't let them know why, not yet," Yann instructed. "If they discover that we've lost the Book, they will waste precious time shouting, panicking, blaming people and arguing about what to do ... just like we did at the start ... and we will lose this small chance to get the clue back."

As Sapphire crouched down for Helen to climb up with Catesby in her arms and the squashed first aid kit on her back, Yann trotted up to them. Helen turned to face him.

"Catesby, my friend. If we challenge the Master again and lose, he will not let us live. Let the human girl heal you and then tomorrow, when you wake, if we are not safe in our beds and the Book is not safe in its box, tell our families what we did and how we failed. Then see if they can do any better." Yann stroked the bird's coppery head. He looked at Helen.

"Healer's child. You ..." He stopped.

Helen said, "I'll fix Catesby. Tell me anything else tomorrow. Good luck."

Rona gave her a hug. Helen said, "We still have to write the end to our song. Let's do that tomorrow."

Lavender wept on her shoulder, but Helen soothed her, "Shhh. I'll see you all soon."

She mounted the dragon and they took off into the night sky. As they flew over the narrow strip of woodland, she squinted through the drizzle and saw the dark shapes of her friends move off in different directions, looking for the one they feared the most.

Chapter 16

Sapphire landed in the field just behind the house. Helen slid down awkwardly, trying not to jostle the injured phoenix, then walked to Sapphire's head and said, "Good luck."

Sapphire blew some silver sparks out of her nostrils and nodded gravely. Helen stood back to give the dragon space and watched as she launched into the air and took off to the west.

Helen approached her house very carefully. Would anyone realize she was missing? She checked her watch and was amazed to see that the journeys to and from the well, and the battle there, had only taken a couple of hours. It wasn't even her usual bedtime yet. But that meant that her Mum and Dad were still up, and it would be difficult to use the surgery in the house.

She could see light coming from the living room window and her Dad's computer room. She clambered over the fence, went up to his window and peered in. He was working calmly, so there was no panic; they thought she was in bed.

She tried the front door, usually opened only for visitors and patients as it led into a tiny waiting room and the small animal surgery. It was locked from the inside. Next, she moved to the dark window of the surgery, where she knew she would find books with detailed instructions on how to splint a bird's wing.

The room often smelt of damp dog, so her Mum sometimes left the window open just a crack. Helen prodded the base of the window. There was a tiny gap. At last, thought Helen, a bit of luck tonight.

She placed Catesby gently on a nearby garden bench, pushed her fingers through the opening and forced the window up. Putting Catesby onto the inside window sill, she squeezed herself through.

She didn't dare switch the light on, so to find the books she needed and to examine Catesby's wing more carefully, she used the torch that her Mum shone down animals' throats.

Now she needed a splint and some tape that wouldn't damage his feathers, but most of her Mum's supplies were in the large animal surgery. She didn't want to move Catesby again, so she made him comfy on her Mum's leather chair and whispered, "I'm leaving you here for a couple of minutes. I have to get a proper splint from the other surgery."

Catesby nodded his head and pecked gently at her fingers.

Taking her Mum's set of keys out of the coat on the back of the door, she climbed out of the window and crept round the house to the large animal surgery, wondering what her friends were doing. Once she had fixed Catesby, she didn't want to go to bed. She wanted to help. But how could she track down a Minotaur? Perhaps if she waited until her Dad was in bed, she could go online and see if any weird and wonderful websites were reporting Minotaur sightings in southern Scotland.

The large animal surgery door was unlocked and slightly open. Her Mum probably hadn't slammed it hard enough. She opened the door very quietly and turned to close it carefully. She jerked it until she heard it click, then reached out her hand to switch on the lights. Blinking in the brightness, she turned to face the large space. Which cupboard were the splints in?

But there, in the centre of the concrete floor, was the largest animal the room had ever held. The Master of the Maze was standing looking at her.

Helen stood totally still and stared back. She felt suddenly cold and very alone. She had no Yann looming behind her, no Rona nor Lavender at her side. She was alone ... with this monster in front of her.

In the bright white room, the Minotaur looked twice the size and twice as dark as he had in the open evening air. His horns almost reached the ceiling. His massive shoulders spanned the room.

His head was dark, with long black curls between his ears, and the skin on his arms and chest, although pale like Helen's, was covered in swirls of rough black hair.

He wore black leather trousers and had bare feet with long curved nails.

From one of his huge hands dangled a bright pink teddy. Nicola's teddy.

"Girl." He spoke in a deep, distorted voice, that sounded painful in his throat.

It was a bull's head speaking, she realized, not a human head like Yann or Rona, or even Frass, had. The Master had the head, throat and mouth of an animal. Yet he forced himself to speak.

"Girl. You must heal me."

"No." She found her own voice, though it was very faint.

"No? Is it right to choose whom to heal? Should you not use your gifts to help everyone who needs you? Do your healers not take a vow to help everyone? Or do you require payment?"

"I don't require anything from you."

"Would threats work better?"

He held Nicola's teddy up to his huge mouth and put its ear delicately between his enormous teeth. Teeth that did not look like a grass-eater's teeth. Teeth that could crush bones.

"Frass brought me this pretty, but he could bring me the baby too, if you refuse me."

Nicola couldn't go to sleep without her pink bear. If the Master had the bear, then one of his creatures had been in the nursery while Nicola was asleep.

Helen thought of Lavender and the words she had read from the clue. 'Brothers and sisters.' Did they have to sacrifice their brothers and sisters to get the Book back? There were millions of books in the world but she only had one sister.

"I'll heal you, if I can," Helen said quietly. Then added, in a more confident voice, "But only if you give me the clue."

"Ha! You gave *me* the clue when you and your little friends couldn't hold on to it." His hand patted the back pocket of his trousers. "You do not make demands of me, girl. You will heal me now or I will send for your sister."

Now Helen knew he had the clue with him, she needed to get closer. "What needs to be healed?"

"My ear."

She looked more carefully at his head. His right ear, just below his huge horn, was ripped and hanging off. She bit on her lips to stop a smile.

"Yann did that!"

"Yes. And he will pay for it when I have the power of the Book. But first I want you to sew it back, as you sewed the colt's leg."

"It will hurt."

"I can stand pain."

More macho nonsense, thought Helen, but pulled a stool over to him.

"I need to look closely at it," she said.

She climbed onto the stool and, as she did so, put out a hand to steady herself, brushing against his back pocket to see if the clue was in there.

The Master grabbed her arm and lifted her easily into the air. He whispered hoarsely, "I will check that I still have the riddle before I leave here." He swung her in time to his slow words. "If you try to steal it, I will make your whole family suffer. Do you understand? Now, girl, sew up my ear." He opened his fist on the last word, and dropped Helen onto the concrete floor.

Helen stifled her cry of pain and shock, not wanting to disturb her parents in the house next door. She took a deep breath and thought quickly about whether she should agree to heal him, even if she couldn't get the clue in return.

If she did as this monster asked, would she be doing it for her own safety or for Nicola's? If she did more than he asked, would she be doing it for her friends, or for the Book? Or to prevent some terrible war she didn't really understand?

She nodded, more to herself than to the Minotaur, then clambered to her feet and moved over to the shelves to collect needles and sutures. She had made no vows, nor taken any ethics courses, so it was an easy decision not to clean his wound first. Let him take his chances, she thought. She walked up to him again, her back straight and her chin up. She would not show him what she was feeling, and she must not show him what she was thinking.

"Good girl," he sneered.

The Minotaur didn't stink like the fauns did, but there was a heat in the air around him, and a pulsing thumping sound, almost as if you could hear his heart. Or perhaps Helen was hearing her own heart as she got nearer the monster.

His eyes were fixed on her, and were set wide apart on the sides of his massive skull. They weren't calm and round like cows' eyes, but had a more oval human shape, with the yellowy white eyeball showing all round the golden orange iris. The rim of the eyelids glowed a hot red, as if these human eyes were burning to get out of this animal's head. She wondered if he felt trapped in there.

She didn't want to look at his eyes, because they made her pity him rather than fear him. So she said, "Turn away so I can see your ear." She looked at the long tear and the small piece of skin still holding the ear on. She had to think of it as a problem to solve.

The dangling ear was only inches from his huge curved horns. The horns had looked silver at Carterhaugh, but now Helen saw that they were pale grey and streaky like old horn spoons, darkening at the tips, which had been sharpened to vicious points.

She threaded her needle.

"This will hurt. You must stay still or it will heal unevenly."

"Don't tell me what to do, girl." But he stood still as she sewed.

Piercing holes in his tough skin, Helen tugged the curved needle through and knotted the thread. She briefly considered making it ragged and squint, but didn't think having an ear at an odd angle would dent his plans for world domination. So she simply carried on, intent on doing as good a job as she could.

Halfway along the wound, sweating from the heat of his skin and the effort of raising her arms above her head to reach the top of his ear, she said, "I'm hot, excuse me," and got down to take off her jumper and remove her watch from her wrist. Then she climbed back up and finished the operation.

He didn't flinch once or make a sound as she sewed.

But when she announced, "Finished," the Minotaur

growled, "If anyone else had hurt me that much, I would have torn them to pieces. Bring me a mirror!"

Sighing with relief that she hadn't botched the repair, Helen found a small mirror in the odds and ends drawer and handed it to the Master.

In his huge hand the mirror looked like a piece of broken glass, as he angled it to see the ear.

"Good. Either you lacked the courage to make a mess of it, or you had the good sense to see that being on my side is to your advantage."

"I'm not on your side. Now give me the teddy and please leave."

He laughed, deep and low in his throat. Helen felt the air round her rattle.

"You will never be rid of me. Once I am in power, all those who have thwarted me will bow down to me."

"I won't bow to anyone."

"You will, girl. You will be the first human to pay me homage. But now I have a Book to find. Thank you for your nimble fingers. Have the pretty back ... for now."

He threw the bear at Helen and moved in long strides to the door. Shoving it open, showing none of the care that Helen had, he was gone.

Helen ran to the doorway, to see which direction he took. Over the fence, like they all seemed to, then north across the fields. A mass of fauns emerged from behind the fence and followed him.

Helen realized that she was kneeling on the floor, her whole body shaking, cuddling the pink teddy and letting the light rain cool her down and wash her clean. But she had no time to deal with her terror. She had to splint Catesby. Then she had to track the Master.

She grabbed the supplies she needed, took thirty seconds to tidy up, then left the surgery as quietly as she could. She made sure she locked the door behind her, then ran round the house to the open window and scrambled in.

Fixing a wing was a complex procedure, but she did it almost without thinking as she told Catesby what had happened in the large animal surgery. And when she had reached the end of her story, the splint looked exactly like the one in the book.

After an initial horrified squawk, the phoenix had remained silent as she talked, then gave her a sympathetic rub with his shining head as she described the Minotaur striding out.

Helen smiled at him and said, "If you were a normal bird, I would strap that wing to your body, but if you do heal fast perhaps you want to keep it moving. What do you think, Catesby?"

He tested the wing, flapping round the surgery once, and nodded his satisfaction.

"Now we must tell the others," whispered Helen, "But how?"

They were scattered all over the country looking for possible lairs, and Catesby couldn't fly strongly enough yet to find them all. Helen knew the Minotaur had gone north ... and even better ... she knew how to follow him!

If only she could get the rest of the fabled beasts back together before the Master read the riddle.

Chapter 17

Helen listened at the door of the surgery for a moment. There was no sound in the hall, so she crept out. On the top of the nearest bookshelves was a brass bowl with old matchboxes in it. She reached up and grabbed one, then, on a whim, picked up an old violin case from the bottom shelf.

Then she tiptoed back into her Mum's surgery, and clambered out through the window holding Catesby under her arm.

She climbed quickly up the hill, past the wood where the friends usually met, right to the summit, picking up branches as she went. It wasn't the highest hill in the area but it was the nearest, and speed was the most important thing.

Together Helen and Catesby built a small pile of

sticks and lit it with the matches. It was a struggle to get the first flames burning as the drizzle was still drifting down, but Catesby used his stronger wing to fan the flames, while Helen ran to the clump of trees to fetch drier fuel.

When the fire was as high and as bright as they could make it, Helen picked up the violin case, took out her old three-quarter size violin and started to play as loudly as she could, drowning out the hissing of the rain hitting the flames.

First, she stood still and played the ballad of Tam Linn, which she had glanced at in the library just a few hours before. Then, as her muscles were stiffening after her bruising evening, she strode round the fire, playing the tune she shared with Rona. This time it was longer, with a battle and pain and threats and fear, but there was still no end.

Helen glanced guiltily at the drops of water bouncing off the varnish on the violin. She hoped it would still play strongly and glow healthily when her sister was big enough to play it. But right now she needed the violin's voice, even if it was raining. And she began to bow even faster.

There was a flapping of wings, and Sapphire arrived with Rona on her back. Helen kept playing, with Rona humming beside her, until Yann galloped up too.

"Why have you summoned us, healer's child?"

As the flames died down, she wiped the fiddle dry, laid it carefully in its case, then started to tell them her story.

"The Master was waiting for me in my mother's surgery. He wanted me to sew up a wound in his ear."

"And did you?" Yann interrupted.

"Yes."

"I damaged him and you fixed him?" Yann said incredulously.

"I had to."

"You had to? Why? Did he ask nicely? Did he offer you treasure and power? Did he offer you answers?"

"*No!* He was holding my sister's toy. He was ..."

"He threatened you with a toy? I thought you were stronger than that, human child."

"Shut up, Yann. Shut up and listen to me."

"Why should I listen to you? You traitor! You collaborator!"

Catesby was squawking at Yann and Rona was grabbing his arm.

But he ignored them and came closer to Helen than he had been since they had held the clue together at Carterhaugh. He shouted in her face, "I should never have trusted a human. We will fight the Master and find the Book on our own from now on." And he turned to leave.

"I can find him for you!"

Yann stopped.

Helen spoke softly, almost inaudible through the rain that was getting heavier and heavier. "I have listened to all your stories, Yann. If you will let me finish my story, I can find him for you."

Yann turned back but didn't look at her. He lifted his face to let the rain land on his cheeks and eyelids.

"He threatened my baby sister's life, so I sewed up his ear. But he let me know he still had the clue, and that he hadn't found the Book yet. So, when I was sewing up his ear, I ..."

There was a blur of purple and Lavender appeared beside the hissing fire.

"What have I missed?"

"Your human friend has been using her heroic healing powers on our sworn enemy, and now she's trying to justify herself."

"I just sewed up his ear, Yann. I didn't save his life!"

"Would you have saved his life?" Yann demanded.

"I don't know. Would you stop me saving a life if I could?"

Yann didn't answer.

"Helen! Did he hurt you? Are you alright?" asked Lavender into the awkward quiet.

"Lavender. That feather you gave me ... can you find it again?"

"Of course, it is still part of me."

"Good, because it is now part of the Master's ear too. I sewed it in as I repaired the wound. I watched him as he left the surgery and he went north. If we go north, and if Lavender can find her feather, then *we* can find the Master."

No one spoke. Everyone looked at Yann.

Yann stared at the mud his hooves had churned up. Then he swallowed and looked at Helen. He said, in a quiet voice, "I have regretted my weakness in bringing my wound to you, I have doubted the wisdom of sharing our problems with a human and I have resented seeing my friends admire you. But perhaps some shrewd fate forced me to your door, because without your cleverness and courage we would have failed a thousand times already." He swallowed hard again. "Well done, healer's child. We will do as you suggest and follow him north."

Helen nodded solemnly at Yann, then laughed as Rona and Lavender crashed into her from both sides, giving her delighted hugs and telling her how wonderful she was.

Yann asked, "Where is he, Lavender?"

The fairy floated up from Helen's shoulder, and rotated slowly in the air above their heads, with her eyes closed and her arms limp by her sides. Then she jerked to a sudden stop and pointed. "North. He kept going north."

"How far?"

"Four or five leagues, no more."

"Then I will ride like a two-legged creature, if Sapphire can cope with my hooves."

So Yann clambered awkwardly onto Sapphire's back. Rona and Helen fitted round him with Catesby in Helen's arms. Lavender perched on one of Sapphire's silver horns to whisper directions in her ear.

The heavily laden dragon lumbered into the waterlogged sky, heading north to find the Master in his maze.

Helen found it even less comfortable than usual on Sapphire's back, with Catesby's claws in her arm and Yann sliding around on the slippy wet scales between the dragon's beating wings, knocking into Rona and Helen when Sapphire swerved to follow Lavender's instructions.

Nor was Helen very comfortable with the thought that she was trying very hard to find a creature she never wanted to meet again.

The night started to glow as they flew north. Helen recognised the rocky lump of Arthur's Seat against the bright line of streetlight orange on the horizon.

"That's Edinburgh!" she called over the noise of the flight.

Before they reached the city, Sapphire landed in a field, bumping briefly into a tree on the way down. Yann immediately tumbled off.

"Is he near here?" asked Helen.

"No," whispered Lavender. "He is there!" She pointed to the amber glow.

"The city!" said Rona. "But we never go to the city! There are no places to hide, because all the dark corners are filled with desperate humans. We are warned never to go to the city."

"Well, the Master is there," insisted Lavender.

"I can go," said Helen. "I've been there lots."

"At night?" asked Yann. "On your own?"

"If he's there and the clue's there, I will go and find him."

Yann laughed. "Then we will follow you!"

So they fitted themselves back on the dragon, with Helen now up near Sapphire's head, so she could add her knowledge of Edinburgh to Lavender's connection with the purple feather.

They flew high over the bypass circling the city, over numberless houses and shopping centres on the outskirts, then inwards to the tree-filled squares and elegant roads of the New Town. Finally, they were above Edinburgh Castle. Lavender asked Sapphire to fly round the castle several times.

The castle was lit up against the dark sky. It squatted

on a huge black rock, looming over the modern shops of Princes Street to the north and the winding maze of the Old Town to the east.

Lavender pointed to the Old Town; the rows of tall, many-windowed buildings piled higgledy-piggledy on the hill sloping down from the castle. "He is in there, somewhere."

Helen guided the dragon down to land in Princes Street Gardens, below the castle. Sheltered under the trees, they decided that Sapphire would have to stay out of sight in the gardens, because she could hardly be hidden on open streets, but they hoped that it was too late, dark and wet for Yann, Catesby and Lavender to be noticed as they searched the city.

Leaving Sapphire in the darkness, they walked past tall statues and clambered over a fence onto a shiny wet city road. Lavender flew on ahead, so intent on her feather she hardly noticed if her friends were behind her. The others followed up the curving road towards the tallest buildings.

Suddenly a hand shot out from a doorway and grabbed Helen's sleeve. She gave a startled yell and yanked herself away. "Gie me a shotty on yir donkey, love," croaked the man crouching on the step.

"Not tonight, mate," she muttered and they accelerated up the hill.

Rona giggled and whispered, "Donkey? You might need to spend more time grooming, Yann!"

Lavender led them into a dark space between two buildings and up a smelly set of stone steps. They turned sharply into a courtyard with high walls rising up all round them, and faint streetlight reflecting off dozens of small windows. Catesby stretched his healing wing, circling slowly up and peering through the glass.

"Why would he be here?" asked Rona, "This is no place for a fabled beast to hide."

"He isn't up here," said Lavender, "He is down there." She pointed to the ground.

"Down where?" asked Yann impatiently.

But Helen nodded slowly. "There are cellars and tunnels all over the Old Town. I did a tour with my Dad last summer. The hill these houses are built on is soft sandstone, and when people got crowded or needed storage space in the olden days, they just dug into the hill. Not downwards, but inwards, because the houses are built right on the side of the steep ridge. Most of the cellars and vaults are closed up now, but he might have found a way in."

"Is his entrance in this courtyard, Lavender?" asked Yann.

"I don't know. I just know he is under us."

"The entrance won't be here," Helen said. "If the cellars are built inwards, then the cellars under our feet will have entrances in the buildings lower down the hill. You stay here, I'll look around."

"I'll come too," offered Yann.

"No, Yann, I'll go with her," said Rona. "I won't be mistaken for a donkey!"

Yann, Catesby and Lavender hid in the darkest corner of the court, while Helen and Rona went back down the stone steps.

They went a short way down the main street and up the next close. It was pitch black and the girls reached out to each other, holding hands as they felt their way along the walls. At the top they found another small courtyard, lower than the one they had left the others in.

By the dim glow of reflected street lights, they saw piles of stone blocks and a small concrete mixer. There were wire fences, decorated with signs about hard hats, blocking off an open door into the bottom storey of a high grey building with no lights at its many windows.

The girls retraced their steps and took Lavender and the others quietly to the building site.

"Yes," said Lavender, her voice abrupt. "He is in there."

So they squeezed between sections of the wire fencing, stepped round bags of cement and coils of cables and went in the open door. They all stopped for a moment, relieved to be dry.

The door led to stairs: a wide clean set of steps heading upwards, and a narrow dingy set of steps leading down. Helen led them downwards, and after twenty or so steps found herself facing a narrow door. Once they were all crowded in front of it, she pushed it open and moved cautiously into the space beyond. Yann had to duck and breathe in, to squeeze through the door behind her.

When Lavender swirled a few light balls into the cold dark room, Helen saw three doorways. "Which way now?"

Rona went down on her hands and knees and sniffed. "That way." She pointed to a door on the left.

She saw Helen looking curiously at her and smiled, showing her sharp little teeth. "Seals have a good sense of smell, though usually we track fish not fauns."

They went further in, through half a dozen rooms with small doors, low ceilings and cracked walls showing bare stone under crumbling plaster. There were no windows in any of these rooms, no fireplaces either; they were just damp spaces hacked roughly out of cold ground. Although there was no furniture, Helen saw that some of the rooms had square cupboards chipped out of the walls. One of them held two old candles, stuck in their own wax.

The dusty stone floor was uneven and Yann kept tripping over his hooves. "Can you put some light balls lower, Lavender, or I'm going to break a leg," he muttered. The purple fairy flicked her wand and a couple of light balls floated down to bounce and roll along the floor, so they could see where to put their feet.

Helen pushed past a rotten wooden door hanging off its hinges, into a larger room with a choice of two doors. Rona sniffed and shrugged. Everyone looked at Lavender. She rotated a few times in the air, then slowed down and sank to the ground. She shook her head and burst into tears. "He seems to be everywhere. The rock is reflecting the magic around and I can't see anything clearly. I'm so sorry."

Helen held her hand out to the fairy and said soothingly, "Calm down. We're in the right place. You've brought us this far, we'll find him. Just be calm."

Yann said, less gently, "At least tell us if he is near. Are we in danger yet? You have to tell us!"

Helen shook her head at him and stroked Lavender's long hair. The fairy said, "I can try to get it outside my head. Then it might make more sense. Hold on."

She screwed her tiny face up in concentration, moved her lips in a silent spell and waved her wand. The dust that their feet had disturbed on the dirt floor began to lift and swirl, creating patterns in mid-air. But just as Helen was starting to see a picture in front of her, Yann sneezed, and the dust shapes exploded.

Lavender stamped her foot on Helen's palm and glared at Yann.

"Sorry!"

The fairy used her wand to gather the dust again and they all held their breath as it settled into lines and shapes in the air. Helen peered at the shifting, shimmering sculpture in front of her, seeing lots of irregular boxes piled in heaps and rows.

Suddenly, she realized that it was a model of the tunnels around them. The room they were in was at the centre, with rooms and tunnels to either side, two layers of tunnels above them, and one layer, partly filled in, below them.

It was like the most complicated 3D chess board she had ever seen; a secret city of cellars and vaults.

And in a dusty box, one layer above them and further in towards the centre of the hill, was a purple glow.

"That's him," pointed Lavender. "That's where he is. We need to go on to the left and up. And we need to be very, very quiet."

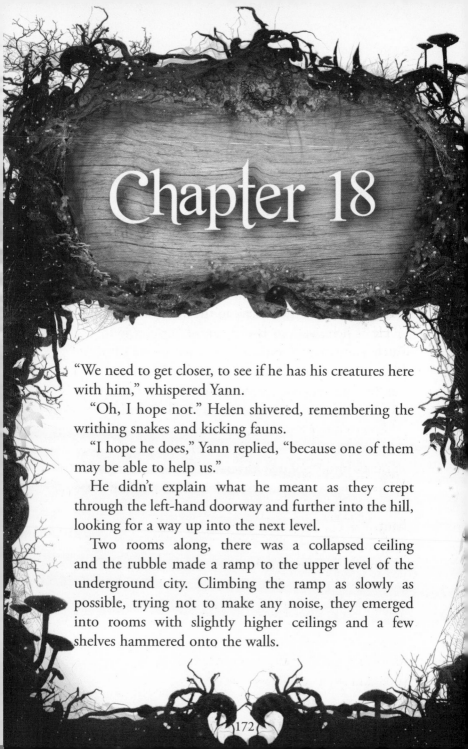

Chapter 18

"We need to get closer, to see if he has his creatures here with him," whispered Yann.

"Oh, I hope not." Helen shivered, remembering the writhing snakes and kicking fauns.

"I hope he does," Yann replied, "because one of them may be able to help us."

He didn't explain what he meant as they crept through the left-hand doorway and further into the hill, looking for a way up into the next level.

Two rooms along, there was a collapsed ceiling and the rubble made a ramp to the upper level of the underground city. Climbing the ramp as slowly as possible, trying not to make any noise, they emerged into rooms with slightly higher ceilings and a few shelves hammered onto the walls.

They moved one step at a time, peering round every doorway, not wanting to walk straight into the Master or any of his court.

Suddenly, they heard a booming noise, followed by hoarse shouting.

"Doesn't *anyone* understand it? Are you *all* fools? Can *no one* unriddle this for me?"

Then the booming started again. Helen wondered if it was a foot kicking a door, or a hand slapping a wall. It was certainly the Master, frustrated and angry, and that meant they were not too late. But how could they get the clue for themselves?

Yann beckoned them back to the previous room.

"He is here, and so is the clue. I can get it for us. Watch and do not interfere." He took a small white object from the pouch hung round his waist, and held it in his right hand.

"The tooth," Helen murmured.

"The tooth of the creature that bit me," he agreed. "We just have to hope the Master still has the little beggar near him."

Then Yann spat on the tooth and waved it in small circles in front of him, muttering a harsh monotonous chant.

Nothing happened.

Yann drew larger circles, and chanted faster. There was a scrabbling sound from the room they had just left. Rona jerked forward, but Yann held up his left hand and waved her back.

Then a weasel came into the room. It entered sideways, its feet sliding out from under it, its teeth bared and its eyes wide open in fear.

The weasel was moving in the strangest way, sliding along the flat floor towards Yann as if it were falling down a steep slope.

Helen had to take a step backwards to get out of the weasel's path, as it seemed not to notice any obstacle in its way. As she moved back, she saw that the animal's paws were bleeding from being dragged across the stone floor.

The weasel finally shuddered to a halt, crushed against one of Yann's hooves.

"Get me the clue. Bring it to me now, without being seen." The weasel whined and wriggled.

"You are in my power and you will do my bidding. Bring me the clue."

Yann lifted the tooth high into the air and the weasel shot out of the room like an arrow from a bow.

Lavender said grimly, "What magic is this, centaur?"

"It is magic that will lead us to the Book."

"It is magic that we are not permitted. It is possession. Who gave you this power?"

Yann answered, through tight teeth and narrow lips, "I won this power. When you were fighting seagulls, I went into the deep dark trees and found some of the ancients. I fought and won a duel and, as my prize, I requested this spell. You can make powerful magic from a tooth of a creature that bit you."

Helen tasted blood on her tongue. She had bitten her lip. The weasel pushing and pulling against itself reminded her of films she'd seen of caged animals in laboratories, driven mad by electrodes in their brains. She realized that she knew very little about her new friends, about their rules and their beliefs. Was she right to pick sides in a battle when she didn't really know what they were fighting for?

She turned to walk away, but Rona put her hand on Helen's arm. Rona's face was pale. "Don't judge us. Please. Don't judge us yet."

Before Helen could respond, there was the faint sound of scratching coming down the tunnel. The weasel slunk into the room, so low to the ground it was like a snake. It had the roll of hide in its mouth, dragging it along like a dead rabbit. It dropped the clue at Yann's hooves and cowered away.

Catesby flew down awkwardly, picked the leather parchment up and gave it to Yann, who unrolled it slightly and nodded.

They all looked at the weasel. It was writhing in pain, trying to back away from the centaur, but it was pinned to the ground by a power no one could see. Yann lifted his front hoof and Helen stepped forward, thinking he was going to stamp on the animal.

Yann turned to her, his face twisted in disgust, sweat sliding down his cheeks. "Back off, girl," he ordered.

Helen held his eye, took two more steps over to the shaking weasel and stood astride it, protecting it with her body.

Yann shook his head very slightly. Then he dropped the tooth on the stone floor and ground it into grit with his heavy hoof.

The weasel collapsed in a pile of fur. Helen bent to touch it and felt its narrow ribcage vibrate. "It's still alive."

Yann closed his eyes for a moment. "No power is worth that price."

Catesby cawed sharply and Yann replied, "I will hear you later, friend, but now we have the clue and we must get out of the Master's maze before he misses it."

They crept back to the top of the ramp leading to the lower rooms, each of them unwilling to look the others in the face. Helen was just about to step onto the rubble when the walls reverberated with a roar of anger.

Four feet and four hooves slid down in an avalanche of stone and plaster, with a flurry of wings battering eyes and heads. They landed hard at the bottom of the ramp, and leapt up to run as quickly as possible through the tunnel.

They heard the noise of a chase behind them. Wordless shouts, footsteps and hoofbeats.

"Move," panted Yann. "Just get out."

The centaur could have galloped past the others and got out well ahead of any creature behind him, but he stayed at the back and urged the rest on. Helen found herself at the front, running as fast as she ever had, trying to remember the way they had come in, trying to follow confused instructions yelled from behind her.

"Go right," screamed Lavender.

"No ... left then straight on," shouted Rona.

Catesby squawked instructions too, but no one bothered to explain them to Helen if they didn't agree with them.

They crashed noisily through dark rooms they had crept carefully through before. They were moving too fast for Lavender's light balls to keep up, so Helen was running in the dark, bumping into walls and corners.

Suddenly she heard her running footsteps echo all around her. She stopped and Rona banged into her back. Lavender hurled some light balls ahead of them, revealing a large chamber, much bigger than any room they had passed through on their way in.

Helen started running again, heading for a closed door at the other side of the chamber, barely noticing the faded murals on the walls and the carved ceilings above. This hadn't been a storage room or a home for poor city dwellers.

She reached the wooden door and pushed it. It moved a few centimetres then stuck. She threw herself against it. It wouldn't move any further. She looked round. The only other exit was the doorway they had come in. And that doorway was now filled with the stooping form of the Master.

"I can't open the door," she said desperately.

"Let me try." Yann pushed past her.

He shoved with his horse and human shoulders and the door scraped open a little more. But the Master was striding towards them, laughing. Several panting fauns were trotting behind him.

"I need more time to open this!" Yann called, shoving again.

Helen stepped forward, towards the Master. She had no idea what she was going to do, as she swung the first aid kit off her back.

There was a blur of ungainly feathers past her left ear, and Catesby flew at the Master's head.

The Master flicked his hand at the bird and tossed him high into the air, but Catesby swooped down again.

This time, as he got near to the bull's black head, his

feathers began to glow, gold and orange and copper. His tail feathers began to spark and he screamed a high-pitched song.

Helen heard Yann shout, "*No!*" as he galloped past her to the bird.

In an instant, the phoenix burst into flames, right in the bull's face.

The Master bellowed, as the bird wove a trail of fire round his head, round his horns, setting his curly hair alight. There was a puff of purple from the bull's right ear and a small scream from Lavender. Then the shape of the phoenix melted into a ball of heat, which suddenly dropped out of the air; an egg laid by a bird of flame.

Helen was forced back by the heat, but Yann dashed forward and caught the glowing egg before it hit the ground. "Farewell, friend," he whispered, as he placed the egg gently in his pouch.

Yann cantered back to the door and, with one enraged shove, pushed it half open.

While the fauns panicked round their Master, flapping their arms to put out the flames on his head, the remaining friends slipped through the door.

The door had been blocked by cardboard boxes. Ordinary twenty-first century cardboard boxes.

They were standing in a storeroom, with a set of wooden stairs leading upwards. Rona went first, a pale and shaking Lavender clinging to her hair. Then Yann scrambled up, while Helen closed the storeroom door and pushed the heaviest boxes back against it.

As Yann reached the top with his front hooves, the steps under his back hooves cracked and the staircase collapsed.

Yann leapt to the top and looked down at Helen. She could hear voices on the other side of the door. The staircase was now a pile of broken planks, with dirty clouds of dust rising from it. The centaur looked horrified. "I'm sorry. I should have gone last. Build a pile of boxes and climb up."

"The boxes are holding the door shut. I can't move them." Helen looked round, trying to slow her breathing down and think of a way to get up and out before the door opened.

Yann called to her, "I'll jump back down, then you can climb on my back and get out."

"Don't be daft. Then you'd be trapped."

Having seen no useful stepladders or grappling hooks in the store room, Helen looked more carefully at the pile of splintered stairs. There was one long narrow piece of unbroken wood ... the bannister that had run up the side of the staircase. She hauled it out and pushed one end up to Yann.

"Can you hold that steady on the edge of the floor? I'm going to try and balance on it."

Yann put his hoof on the end of the rail and nodded to her.

As she wedged her end carefully in the heap of dusty debris, she heard banging at the door behind her. But she couldn't rush. She put her left foot on the narrow beam and began to lift her right foot. The wood was narrower than the sole of her boot. Would it take her weight? The wood creaked and bent slightly ... but it didn't break.

She looked up at Yann. "Please don't sneeze!"

"Just come on!"

Holding her arms out for balance, she took small steps. She could hear the barrier of boxes slithering slowly along the stone floor behind her. She took another couple of steps, refusing to look behind her, concentrating her eyes and her mind on her feet.

Yann called out, "Healer's child." She glanced up. Yann had bent his forelegs and was reaching both arms down for her. She wobbled as she shifted her balance to twist her arms up, then they grabbed each other's wrists and Yann swung her up to land in a heap at his hooves. He reached down to pull the bannister off the cellar floor, so no one else could use it.

Helen looked round. She was in a room lit by street lights shining through a big window, surrounded by shelves, stools and mirrors, and row upon row of shoes and boots. She laughed out loud. She'd bought wellies in here once.

Rona was pushing at the door out onto the street. "It's locked!" Helen went behind the till to look for a key, but then they heard a triumphant yell from below. The Master's creatures had got through the door. Without hesitating, Yann reared up on his hind legs and smashed his front hooves through the shop window. Glass flew everywhere, sparkling on the leather boots and Christmas trees in the window display.

An alarm went off instantly, drowning out the noise from the storeroom. Yann was already on the pavement, as Rona and Helen clattered out over the glass and shoes into Cockburn Street.

"Which way?" asked Yann.

Helen pointed downhill. "We need to get back to Sapphire."

The streets were still shiny and wet from the rain, but the clouds had blown over and there were a few stars visible in the sky.

They ran, Yann's hooves echoing off the buildings as they hurtled down the winding street, slowing at the sharp bends, so they didn't slip on the wet cobbles. Helen slid to a halt at the bottom so she could get her bearings. She felt a tug on her back, screamed and turned round with a kick and an elbow.

Yann leapt sideways. "Sorry, I didn't mean to startle you. I was just putting the clue in your rucksack. You must guard it. Sapphire can't fly safely and fast with me on her back, so you must go without me and find the Book. I will outpace the Master and his creatures on the ground."

"How will you get out of the city?" asked Helen.

"I'll go north first, to stretch my legs and leave those trotting fauns behind me. But then ..." he glanced up at the stars clear in the sky, "then I will let the stars guide me south again. I'll find open ground eventually."

Rona gave Yann a quick hug, and Lavender blew him a kiss, but Helen stood back and simply said, "Good luck." He nodded to her and galloped off, heading past Waverley Station.

Helen, Rona and Lavender listened as his hoofbeats got fainter. Then they heard other, smaller, hooves and set off at a run for the gardens.

They shoved each other over the fence and tumbled down the hill to the trees. Sapphire appeared silently and crouched down for them to climb on. She took off just as a dark crowd swarmed down the hill towards them.

Sapphire flew over the city for quarter of an hour searching for Yann, but no one could see him or hear his hooves. Either he had got away very fast, thought Helen, or he was hiding in a dark corner. Or perhaps he hadn't outpaced the Master after all.

Chapter 19

Sapphire returned to the field south of Edinburgh where they had landed just a couple of hours before. They clambered off and squatted on the dry grass under the trees.

Rona told the dragon the story of how Lavender's magic found the Master, Yann's magic forced the weasel, and Catesby's bravery let them escape. Sapphire sighed small puffs of smoke, scratching the earth with her claws as the story went on.

When Rona described Yann galloping off, carrying Catesby's egg, perhaps pursued by the Master's creatures, the story felt unfinished, but they didn't have any more to tell.

Helen asked, "What did Catesby actually do?"

Lavender explained. "Phoenixes can burn and then

rise from the ashes, but they can only hatch seven times. So Catesby has given one of his lives to get us out of the Master's maze. But he may not hatch again for a long time; not in time to find the Book, not in time to come to the Solstice Gathering ... perhaps not while we are still young. He is Yann's best friend, and now Yann may be a grey mane before he can talk to Catesby about tonight, and ask his forgiveness for the way he twisted magic to get that weasel to bring us the clue."

Sapphire growled a question and Lavender answered, "I don't know where the Master is now. I felt my feather burn when Catesby burst into flames. We are no longer connected."

"Oh no!" exclaimed Helen. "Now we don't know if he's nearby. He could ambush us again."

"Well, *I'm* delighted I can't feel him anymore," said Lavender, "I felt ill all the time that I was part of him."

"I'm sorry. I didn't think of that when I sewed the feather in."

"We got the clue back. That's what matters."

But they were all thinking about Yann and Catesby. They mattered too.

"Let's read the clue," suggested Rona. "Let's try to finish this now. We must have the Book back by tomorrow evening and if we have to travel far to fetch it, we had better start now."

Helen opened her green bag and pulled out the battered piece of leather. Two holes in it had been repaired with tiny red stitches.

Lavender cast a clear white light on the words written on the leather in dark brown ink.

I line up with my brothers and sisters,
Watched over by the stone eyes of my
father and mother.

Helen sighed. "Another riddle. Why couldn't the Book just draw us a map? Will we have to go to the library again to work this one out?"

"Perhaps!" exclaimed Lavender. "Perhaps that is the very place."

The other three looked at her expectantly.

The fairy grinned. "The Book crafted this riddle. What are a book's mother and father?"

"The people who wrote it?" asked Helen. "Which in this case are the wizard and fairy who loved unanswerable questions. But they're both dead, aren't they?"

"Yes, long ago."

"Long enough ago for them to be fossils and have stone eyes? That seems unlikely."

"What are a book's brothers and sisters?" Lavender asked.

Rona shrugged. "Other books?"

Helen said impatiently, "Lavender, what do you know?"

"In your hall of books, in your building of learning, I met all those stone heads. One of them, a bearded man in a cloak of stars, had a tiny fairy on his shoulder. I wanted to ask you about him but you found Tam Linn and I forgot. Could he be the wizard who wrote the book?"

"But why would he be in my school? Was he a headmaster or a local poet, like all the other busts?"

"Wizards travel among humans in many guises. Who can say what he was to the people of Clovenshaws?"

185

"So if he is the father and the fairy is the mother, then the line of brothers and sisters must be the books on the shelves of the school library! We've been using the library to follow the Book's clues, and the Book's been there all the time." Helen put her head down on her knees and groaned.

"The Book has been testing us," said Rona. "How better to do it than to watch us unravel its clues?"

Helen looked up again. "But how could the Book know that Yann would come to me with his cut leg, or that I would use the school library to help you?"

"The Book knows all the answers," said Rona serenely. Helen groaned again.

"So, how do we get into your school to find the Book?" said Lavender briskly.

"We don't. Not tonight." Helen thought of the broken glass and scattered shoes in the shop. "We aren't going to break in and damage anything. I'm sure the Book wouldn't appreciate that. We'll go in tomorrow, nice and quietly, when the school opens, and invite the Book to leave its brothers and sisters and go home with you."

After retrieving her old fiddle from the hill, Helen put the case and the first aid kit in the garage, and took out the longest ladder she could find. With Rona's help she manoeuvred it round the house to her bedroom window.

Hugging Rona goodbye, she climbed stiffly up the ladder and shoved at the window. But it was shut fast.

Someone had locked it from the inside. Someone had been in her room and discovered that she wasn't there.

Sighing, she slid down the ladder, and walked reluctantly to the back door. Her Mum was sitting at the long kitchen table, with a book open in front of her and a mug of cold coffee in her hand.

Helen walked in and sat down at the other end of the table. Her Mum pointed to the kitchen clock. It was three in the morning.

She said calmly, "Where have you been? What have you been doing?"

Helen thought of all the lies she could tell. But none of them were convincing.

"I've been with some friends. Helping them with a problem."

"Was that what you were doing last night too?"

Helen nodded. "Yes. I'm sorry."

"It's the middle of winter. It's pitch black out there. It just isn't safe to be wandering around when I think you're in your bed. What kind of trouble are your friends in?"

"I can't tell you."

"Is it illegal?"

"No."

"Is it to do with ..." her Mum's calm voice wavered. "Oh Helen, is it to do with smoking, or drinking, or drugs, or motorbikes?"

"No, none of those things."

"Is it to do with boys?"

Helen briefly considered whether Yann was a boy, and decided four legs and a tail meant he wasn't a boy as her Mum would understand it.

"It isn't about boys."

"Is it some spooky nonsense like ouija boards, or that bonfire on the hill this evening?"

Helen thought about the real, physical presence of the Master in the surgery and the teddy in his mouth, and said carefully, "No, Mum, it is not some spooky nonsense like ouija boards."

"Is it ...? This is ridiculous! We are not playing twenty questions all night. You will tell me where you have been, who you have been with and what you have been doing. Or you will lose all your privileges and will have to stay in the house and garden just like Nicola."

"I can't tell you."

"I have been so scared. Your Dad's been sitting with Nicola since she developed a temperature earlier, so I've been here all alone since midnight, wondering if you were at the bottom of the Tweed or run over by a car. But I couldn't call the police or the rescue team again because this time I thought you were lost on purpose. You *will* tell me what you have been doing. Now!"

"I'm sorry, but I can't tell you, Mum."

Helen saw a flicker of movement at the kitchen window, and thought immediately of the final clue, now folded up inside her fleece. Had the Master come back? She had to get her Mum out of danger. "Mum, please can we talk about this in the morning? I'm a bit too tired just now."

Her Mum stood up and kicked her own chair across the kitchen.

The crash broke the calm and quiet, and now she was shouting. "Don't you try to dismiss me, young lady. If you are too tired to have a discussion now, then you should have got a good night's sleep instead of spending the night wandering about the countryside. Tell me what you have been doing. Tell me now."

Helen tried not to glance at the window again, and kept her voice soft. "I am very sorry that I went out without permission. But I can't tell you." Helen stood up.

"Right. That's it!" her Mum yelled. "You are grounded from now on. You will not be going out with any friends, or to any films or parties over Christmas. Nor well into next year."

"Can I go to school?"

"Don't be cheeky! Of course you can go to school. But you won't be going anywhere else for a while. Now up to bed, and don't you *dare* leave your room again."

"I'll just get a drink of water. I'll be up in a minute."

Her Mum stood watching Helen as she poured a glass of water, then took some very slow sips. Her Mum sighed heavily and strode out of the room without another word.

Helen waited until her Mum was upstairs, then she got the bread knife out of the dishwasher and went quietly to the back door. She jerked the door open and stood there with the knife held out in front of her.

In the doorway was a familiar shape.

"Yann! Are you alright?" she whispered.

"I'm fine. Was that your mother?"

"Yes. She's a bit annoyed."

"I'm ashamed to say that I overheard. You did not betray us when she asked you to."

"No. She just needed to shout at me and I had to let her."

"I never talk to my father now without him shouting at me. Is it like this for everyone? Catesby's no help about parents, because his parents are both eggs at the moment, so he gets on fine with them."

"Parents are harder to deal with than monsters. You have to love them as well as fight with them."

"Yes," agreed Yann, "and you can't just kick them and run away either."

"Tempting thought," grinned Helen, "but I have nowhere to run to."

"Do you still have the clue?"

"Yes," she wriggled it out from under her fleece and handed it to him, "but we've already worked it out. The Book is in my school library. We'll get it tomorrow morning."

Helen quickly told Yann the plan she and the others had worked out. Yann grunted. "Why can't we just push a window in and get the Book right now? Win it with hoof and tooth and claw."

"Because we need to show a bit of respect for the Book, its family and my school. We'll get it calmly and quietly in the morning and that'll be plenty of time for your Solstice celebrations in the evening."

"But the Master has read the riddle. He could still get there before we do."

"Then keep watch on the library. You told me that the Book took fright when you borrowed it, so don't you think that retrieving it calmly would be a better idea than going in kicking and biting? That weasel certainly wishes it hadn't bitten you."

Yann shied away from her. "You don't understand about the weasel."

"I understand evil more every night I spend with you, Yann. I thought you were on the side of the good guys. But now I'm not so sure."

"So why didn't you betray us to your mother, if you think we are as bad as the Master?" Yann demanded.

"I don't know, Yann. Maybe because the Master enjoys power over others ... and you didn't."

"Don't try to get inside my head, human child, and don't tell me what I can and can't do. I am no one's pet pony!"

Yann stamped his hoof once and galloped off to leap the fence.

On her way to bed, Helen stood for a while at her parents' door, wondering if she should go in and talk to her Mum again. Then she shook her head, whispered, "Night night," and went to bed herself.

Chapter 20

Helen dragged herself awake, stiff, sore and still exhausted. But she had to get up. It was Friday. The Winter Solstice. The quest would end today, in success or failure.

She waited until she heard her Mum go into the shower, then she crept downstairs to make herself breakfast.

Her Dad came in to the bright warm kitchen as she was eating her Gran's apple jelly on toast.

"Dad, I'm so sorry about last night."

"Oh Helen," he sighed and shook his head. "Last night we were so worried about you, and this morning we're very disappointed. I know your Mum has grounded you, so I don't want to go through it all again." He sat down beside her. "But if you need to tell me anything, or ask me anything, then I will always listen, and I will try hard not to judge."

"Thanks, Dad. I might do that."

"Do you want a warm drink before going out in the cold air? It's frosty out there."

"No thanks. I need to rehearse my piece for the concert, then I'll head off to school."

Helen went up to her room, and after a few finger exercises, she played Solstice to herself. It was nearly finished but there was a darker edge in it now that she hoped she could balance with a happy ending.

Her Mum was already in the small animal surgery when Helen left for school, and her Dad and a snotty, sneezy Nicola were making patterns on the kitchen table with toast fingers. As she opened the back door, Helen said, "See you soon, I hope."

"Bye, darling," her Dad replied, without looking up.

"Bye bye, Hen." Nicola waved her sticky pink teddy.

It was a clear, cold day. There were no clouds in the pale blue sky and Helen's breath glittered in the air as she strode down the lane. Silver frost glistened on the fence posts and bare bushes, and her feet crunched on shallow icy puddles.

She could see no other living things, but she felt them all around her. Shiftings in hedges and trees. Passing whiffs of singed hair, damp fur and sudden stinks like the zoo on a hot day. And once a tiny squeak, cut off as soon as it started.

Kirsty was waiting for Helen at the end of her lane.

"How are you today?" she said cheerfully, trotting beside her on the grass verge.

"Walk in the middle of the lane," instructed Helen.

"What?"

"Just walk down the centre, not too near the hedges."

"Why?"

"Och, you know, there are some really jaggy bushes round here, and you don't want to rip your jacket. Cold today, isn't it?"

Kirsty joined Helen in the centre of the path and looked oddly at her.

"Do you really want to talk about the weather?"

"No."

They walked in silence towards the school. When they arrived at the playground, the children who came by bus from the furthest farms were there already, their voices sounding very small under the huge bright winter sky.

Helen put her school bag and fiddle case right in the middle of the playground.

"Do me a favour, Kirsty. Stay here with these for a minute."

"Why, do you have the crown jewels in there?"

"Please. I'll just be a minute."

She looked around but couldn't see anything out of the ordinary. No horns, no flicking whipping tails, no sharp teeth, no fairy wings or dragon scales. But she felt a lot of eyes on her.

She walked to the school door, pushed it open and went in, striding down the modern corridors to the door of the old building. It was heavy and stiff, but she shoved it open with her shoulder. There were no lights on. This bit of the school wasn't cleaned as often as the classrooms, and no one had been in here yet. She flicked on all the light switches, not caring about global warming today, walked towards the library, and taking a deep breath, pushed open the door.

She had dreaded seeing chaos and destruction, but the room was as dusty and musty and haphazardly untidy as it always was. Perhaps no one had been here since she had read the story of Tam Linn yesterday lunchtime.

She glanced round the top shelves. There was the bust Lavender had described; a smiling man with a long beard that had never been in fashion, a cloak with stars on it and a tiny figure on his shoulder.

Helen cleared her throat and spoke to the shelves, turning round slowly to address each wall of the library in turn.

"Book. Book of questions and answers. I am here on behalf of the young fabled beasts who took you from your place of safety. They are sorry they disturbed you, and apologize for putting you in danger. They have solved all your riddles and passed most of the tests you set them. They ask now that they might have the honour of returning you to your home, and paying you the respect you deserve tonight at the Winter Solstice celebration. Please."

She paused and looked round the shelves. Nothing happened, not a puff of dust or a shifting page.

"Oh, come on! They've tried really hard!"

Out of the corner of her eye, she saw a slight movement and she whirled round. Everything was still, but under the bust of the wizard, one book was out of alignment, poking just over the edge of the shelf.

Helen moved the unwieldy wooden ladder on wheels and climbed up.

"Thank you," she said and reached out for the Book.

Its silver cover was warm to the touch and she held it gently as she climbed down. She stood at the bottom of the ladder and thought of the answers in the Book. Perhaps in there she could find out why Yann hated humans so much. Perhaps the Book would tell her why she could never do anything that pleased her Mum. Perhaps the end of the piece of music was there, or even exam answers for next term.

She looked at the pearly clasp holding the Book closed, but she didn't touch it. She would find out all these things in good time. Turning her back on the shelves, she faced the door and tightened her grip on the Book. "Here we go. I hope this works."

Helen marched out of the library, along the corridor and into the new school, past Mr Crombie and Mrs Murray, who were chatting outside the staffroom.

"Morning," she said and kept going.

She pushed out of the school door and into the playground. The sky was no longer blue. The air was no longer crisp. A mist had fallen over the village, clinging to everything, subduing the children playing outside. Helen could see only three steps ahead of her.

She walked straight to the hedge between the school grounds and the new village hall. As she reached it, Rona stepped out from between the bushes and held out her hands. Helen put the Book in them, then Rona disappeared.

Almost instantly there were fast hoof-beats in the fog, and a streak of purple and blue in the air. The Book was going home, as fast as Yann's legs could carry it, protected by Sapphire's fire and Lavender's wand.

Helen heard a scurrying and a chattering, a hissing and a growling. Then a disappointed silence. And slowly the mist began to lift.

Kirsty came up, dragging all the bags.

"Who was that? Did I see you with a girl?"

"Yes. But I don't think I'll be seeing her again."

Helen sat down suddenly on the tarmac and hunted in her pockets for a packet of hankies.

Chapter 21

After a long, dull day at school, Helen arrived home bedraggled and sleepy. She had hoped for a sign from the fabled beasts that the Book was safe, but they'd made no plans for a signal nor arrangements to meet, so she was slowly accepting that she may never know what happened next.

She trudged into the kitchen and slung her bags under a chair. On the table was a roll of cream paper, tied by a gold ribbon, with her name in curly letters on the outside. Helen sat down and looked at the parchment warily. Surely it wasn't another riddle? She picked it up, slid the ribbon off the end of the tube, unrolled it and began to read.

She jumped up when her Mum strode through the

back door, slamming it behind her, and flinging the torn, dirty and burnt first aid kit onto the table.

"I found this in the garage. Did you steal it? There are syringes and scalpels missing! What on earth have you been doing with syringes and scalpels?"

Helen didn't try to answer, she just handed her Mum the roll of parchment. Her Mum read out loud:

In grateful recognition of aid given and bravery shown, Yann Smith, Rona Grey, Lavender Flowerdew and Sapphire Spark invite Helen Strang to their Winter Solstice Gathering at ten o'clock tonight. Dress warmly!

We will send transport at nine o'clock.

PS. Thanks especially for the fetlock stitched, the wing splinted, the eyesight restored and the life saved.

Her Mum looked up.

"Is this your explanation for the stolen equipment and the late night walks? These friends – Yann, Rona,

Lavender and Sapphire – needed your help with some injured animals?"

"Yes. That's about right."

"How did the animals get injured?"

"It was mostly a mad bull."

"That can be nasty. But why did they need you to fix their animals? Why didn't they phone a real vet?"

"They couldn't. Their parents don't approve or something. But I used all the right equipment and copied techniques from your books. And so far everything has healed fine."

"Even the splinted wing? That's hard to do."

"Well, it's a bit difficult to tell with the splinted wing right now, but he did seem to be flying fine last night."

"Well, I think you were very irresponsible to take this on yourself, but I can't really criticize, as I spent half my childhood fixing rabbits and owls and weasels."

Helen shivered at recent memories, as her Mum grinned at old ones.

Her Mum sat down and thought for a moment.

"Oh, alright. I will let you go to this party, but you must promise that if anyone else asks you to provide first aid for an animal, you will consult me as soon as possible."

"As soon as possible, Mum, absolutely. Thanks so much." Her Mum pulled the exotic animals textbook out of the rucksack and flicked through the crumpled pages. "We could look through this together sometime if you want," she said hopefully.

"Yes," smiled Helen. "That might be useful. But ..."

"But not right now. Go and get ready for your party!"

And Helen went upstairs for a long hot bath, and to

get needles and thread from her sewing box, rather than her Mum's surgery.

At five to nine, Helen was ready. She had her own blue rucksack packed with no veterinary equipment whatsoever, and was wearing clean jeans and warm socks.

The doorbell rang at nine o'clock and both her parents went to answer it.

Helen peered round them. Rona was standing on the doorstep, wearing a sleeveless blue dress that shimmered in the light from the hall.

"I'm Rona," she said politely to the Strangs. "I've come to take Helen to our Gathering."

"Of course," said Helen's Mum. "But aren't you freezing in that dress?"

Rona looked at her arms and smiled. "It's fine, I have a layer of fat that keeps me really warm."

Helen tried not to giggle, then she hugged her Mum and Dad. "I'll be back after midnight. Is that okay?"

"So long as someone brings you home."

"We'll get her home, don't worry," said Rona. "We always have."

With the adults watching, Helen and Rona left by the gate, rather than leaping over the fence.

"Thanks for the invitation," Helen said as they walked down the path.

"Oh, we were always going to invite you. We just never got time to do it properly before."

"But thanks especially for the PS. It turns out that Mum will forgive me anything if she thinks I've been helping poor dumb animals. It got me out of a lot of trouble."

Sapphire was waiting in the lane and the girls climbed on. They flew for only quarter of an hour, before landing on the edge of a flat grassy space bordered by a small woodland, a curve of river leading to the sea and a stony beach. The sea and the river were calm on this dry windless night.

Helen looked towards the centre of the clearing. It was filled with moving lights and shadows. There were figures milling around on varying numbers of legs: some walking, some flying, some huge, some so small she could hardly make them out.

"Where are we?" asked Helen.

"A place where all the fabled beasts, from land and sea, from river and tree, can feel at home. We gather here every Solstice, Winter and Summer."

They jumped off Sapphire and were met by Yann and Lavender.

Lavender was wearing a very frilly purple dress and carrying a large wand, bound with ribbons. Yann had several narrow plaits in his hair and had groomed his coat and polished his hooves.

"Tell me about the Book," asked Helen. "Did you get it home safely?"

"Yes, we did," whispered Yann, "but no one else knows, so don't shout about it. Our parents will be bringing out the Book soon, and unless the Book decides to tell of its adventure, we may have escaped punishment."

"Hardly," said Helen. "Every single one of you will have a scar of some kind. Is Catesby still an egg?"

Yann patted the embroidered pouch on his hip gloomily. "Yes."

"So what happens at your Solstice Gathering?"

Rona answered, "First we consult the Book, then some families and tribes dance or sing, or create beauty in other ways. Then we all eat and drink far too much and go to bed very late!"

Helen took off her rucksack. "Well, in my family, we give gifts at this time of year, so I brought you each something."

She pulled four packages from her rucksack.

First she handed Sapphire a hard round package. "So you can see how you look with your necklaces and bracelets on." Sapphire ripped the paper to find a mirror with gemstones round the frame. The dragon held it in her silver claws and admired herself, rumbling a note of deep pleasure.

Then Helen handed Rona a square package. "For singing on rocks." Rona found a book of sea shanties and ballads, and started humming them immediately.

Helen gave Yann another flat package but said nothing as he opened it. He found a hardcover book too, but with blank pages. "Now you can write your own answers," said Helen quietly.

Last, she gave Lavender a tiny soft package and an envelope. Lavender opened the package and out fell a little white dress with pink and blue ribbons. "Oh Helen, it's lovely ... but I can only wear purple." Lavender sounded on the edge of tears.

"Open the envelope."

Out of the envelope fluttered pictures from a

gardening catalogue; varieties of lavender with white, pink and blue flowers.

"You can wear lots of colours, and not lose your Lavender luck."

Lavender squealed, and created a small cylinder of black round herself while she changed quickly into her new dress.

"Thank you, thank you, thank you," she shouted and kissed Helen on the nose.

The others thanked her too, in quieter voices. "We don't have gifts for you," apologized Rona.

"I can watch your celebration and that will be your gift."

They turned towards the centre of the field, nearer the lights and the shifting figures.

But Helen's way was suddenly blocked by a huge white beast.

Its head towered over her, and its powerful legs and hooves forced her backwards.

"Who has brought a human to our secret gathering?"

"I have," said Yann, trotting to Helen's side.

The beast shifted back slightly and Helen saw that this was another centaur. A pure white horse, joined to a man's pale torso and blond head. But he was a chest and head taller than Yann.

"Why is she here?" he demanded, his voice deeper and richer than Yann's. "These creatures have poisoned our land, cut down our woods and built on every inch of good galloping ground. They use our cousins the horses as slaves. Humans are more our enemies than any practitioners of dark magic. Get her away from here, son."

Helen felt all her friends move closer to her.

"Humans are not our enemies, Father. And dark magic is not to be talked of lightly."

Yann spoke in his usual arrogant voice, but Helen heard a quiver that was not normally there. She wasn't sure if she should speak up, try to defend Yann. Then she remembered Yann listening awkwardly to her and her Mum arguing and decided that a human girl getting between him and his father wouldn't help Yann at all.

His father spoke high above them all. "You know little of the world, colt. You do not know how even the most silver-tongued human can betray you."

"I judge this human girl not by what she says but by what she does. And she has never betrayed us. So she will stay with us tonight."

Yann's father took a sudden pace towards him. But Yann stood firm. The huge stallion wound one of Yann's plaits round his fingers and pulled his head up.

"Do you defy me? You will not mix with this kind. You will not risk our people being betrayed and discovered. If you will not remove her, then I will do it myself, with my hooves and my hands."

Sapphire growled gently behind Helen.

The white centaur glanced over. "I am not afraid of dragons, lizard child. I have beaten your father in a fair fight before now and would make easy work of you."

Concerned that this was becoming more than a family disagreement, Helen said softly, "I don't want to cause trouble, Yann. I'll just go home if I'm not wanted."

Yann jerked his head back out of his father's grip.

"No, healer's child. I invited you here, and you are my guest. Please stay. Most other fabled beasts will treat you with courtesy."

He raised his voice to the skies. "Father, she is a healer, a musician and a solver of riddles. This gathering has welcomed bards and adventurers from the human race for millennia. More than that, she is my friend. If I have to, I will fight for her right to be here."

Yann stood as tall as he could, chin up, and looked straight at his father.

The white centaur reared once, his hooves a hair's breadth from his son's face. Yann didn't move.

His father laughed as his hooves touched the ground. "You are growing up, boy. Don't let her run off with any of our treasures."

He turned and walked away, flicking his silvery white tail, and lifting his massive hooves delicately over the long dark grass.

Yann watched him go, his face pale and his chest heaving. When his father was out of sight in the crowd of beasts, he turned to the others and muttered, "Come on, let's go and watch the Book reading."

He started to move away, but Helen touched his arm and he stopped.

She waited until the others were out of earshot.

"Thank you, Yann."

Yann was silent for a few moments. Then he said quietly, "My father is not always right." He grinned at Helen. "Neither am I, but don't tell anyone!"

The two of them followed the others to a small rise in the grass, behind the mass of fur, feathers and scales gathered around a central space. They could see over the fabled beasts' heads to a white stone in the middle of the crowd.

Yann looked around. "If the Book wants to accuse us of rule breaking, then we might be able to make an escape from here."

Helen asked, "You would run away?"

He sighed. "No. We brought the Book back, and no one died. If the Book tells, we will be in a great deal of trouble, but we would see it through. Wouldn't we?"

Lavender looked a bit weepy, but Rona and Sapphire nodded. Then they waited for the Book.

Chapter 22

As Helen watched, a procession emerged from the forest. Leading it was Yann's father, followed by a red dragon, a tall willowy woman with stiff arms, a tiny flickering blue fairy and a short plump woman in shimmering green who looked like Rona.

"Our elders," Rona whispered to Helen. "That's my mum."

They were carrying a carved wooden box, passing it round, always to the right, so that they each held it for a moment. The crowd opened to let them through.

Then Yann's father stood by the shining white stone, opened the box and lifted out the Book that Helen had spoken to only that morning. Placing the Book gently on top of the stone, he opened it and called in a clear, carrying voice:

"A delegation from the western forests wishes to ask the first question. Step forward, Brother."

A low grey form, shaped like a man but with a line of shaggy fur down his back, stepped forward and spoke in a growling voice:

"Honoured Book. The faery queen of the forest folk is sending heralds to prepare the way for her home-coming to the new forests of the west. Those of us who have homes there fear her return and her changeable moods. We question her right to drive us away after so many centuries' absence."

Helen looked at Rona beside her and Rona shrugged.

A sudden wind blew from the sea and rippled the Book's pages. When they settled the centaur read:

"Brother, the Book answers you. Those wooded lands that are hers are hers by ancient right. Those wooded lands that have never been hers, she may covet but she should not take, whether by charm or cunning or force. So there will still be forests you may dwell in, if you can defend them."

The questioner nodded his thanks and slipped away into the crowd.

Then the centaur called out again. "Honoured and Revered Book. The second question. There have been sightings of the Master of the Maze in our lands these last days. Need we fear him and his creatures this winter?"

The pages moved again in a breeze that didn't reach Helen and her friends on the mound. When the paper settled, the glowing white centaur read:

"No, you need not fear him, for this year he has been defeated by the elders of the future and the healer's child."

There was a murmur round the crowd and a cheer started up.

The centaur raised his powerful voice over the noise. "And finally, Honoured Book, is there another question we should ask this year?" Rona whispered to Helen, "If we have a spare question we always ask this, just in case there is anything new we need to know. If the Book wants to reveal its travels and our quest, it will do so now."

Helen felt Rona go tense beside her. She heard Yann take a deep breath and saw Lavender bite her little lip. Sapphire's scales were dull with anxiety.

The pages rippled again, right to the end. Then the wind died down and the pages stopped moving. Yann's father read:

"How do you make amends when you have broken the rules? Fix the damage done, retrieve the things lost and fear the anger of those betrayed."

There was puzzled silence for a moment, then Yann's father and the other elders bowed to the Book, placed it in carefully back in its box and carried it away, whispering among themselves.

Rona and Lavender hugged each other, then both hugged Helen, while Yann gave Sapphire a hearty thump between the wings.

"The Book has forgiven us!" squealed Lavender. "Our punishment was to fear their anger, not to feel it!" She gasped, "Oh, I must go. Our flower dance is the first show!" She flew off as fast as a hawk diving.

"This is a good place to watch Lavender dance. We will stay here," said Yann.

"Do you all perform at the gathering?" asked Helen.

Rona answered, "No. Some families, like Lavender's, practise for months and do really fancy things. Others, like the centaurs, think entertaining a crowd is beneath them!" Rona laughed. "Selkies sometimes sing, but my mum isn't singing this year."

She looked at Helen. "We could perform together though. I saw your fiddle in your bag. You must have thought of playing it here."

Helen watched as dozens of fairies spiralled up from the grass, twisting and spinning like seeds caught on the breeze. She saw Lavender, bright in her white dress, in the midst of many colours.

"I don't think I should play to your families and friends. They don't really like humans, do they?"

"Nonsense. We tell so many stories about humans that most would be fascinated to see a real one close up. Anyway, I can't sing the song without you because we wrote it together, and so much of it is yours alone."

"But won't the song tell everyone about how you lost the Book?"

"No, it is like an olden-days tale; a quest. It won't seem real, will it, Yann?"

"Rona needs to sing before this gathering sometime soon in order to be accepted as a sea-singer by her people." He smiled at the selkie. "But sometimes she's shy! Would you find it easier with the healer's child than on your own?"

Rona objected, "It's not that I'm shy. It's her song too. She asks the questions and she puts the broken bits back when the melody fractures."

Helen said, "I need to play too, at my school concert on Monday, to be accepted for the music school I want to go to next summer." She thought for a moment, then nodded.

So Rona and Helen sat watching the fairies' intricate aerial dance above the white stone, and hummed the tune to each other, finding their way round each other's notes.

When the fairies had finished, and Lavender was back with them, perched breathless on Yann's shoulder, Rona took Helen's hand and Helen grabbed her fiddle. They walked down the small hill to the back of the crowd.

Rona pushed past various beasts and peoples, most of whom Helen couldn't identify, though they avoided the group with the yellow eyes and fur running down their spines. When they reached Rona's mother, Rona whispered to her and the short woman looked briefly at Helen. Then she nodded and turned away again.

Some small bearded men were juggling rocks in the middle of the gathering, and when they had finished, Rona led Helen out into the centre. "Just a moment," Rona said and vanished.

Helen looked round at the circle of faces, large and small, all staring at her; most curious, some hostile. She had a moment of panic.

Then she heard a note from the ground and looked down. Rona was still there but now she was a seal. Helen laughed as she remembered Rona saying she sang better as a seal. This was exactly how their quest song was meant to be performed!

She brought her fiddle to her shoulder and they began. Although they had never actually played the whole piece together, nor rehearsed with Rona as a seal, Rona's high unwavering voice and Helen's soaring music worked perfectly together. They knew the story so well and could still feel the fear of failure, the frustration of the riddles, the pain of battle, the concern for each other and the final relief of success.

This was the perfect place to compose the ending. So they did.

When the quest song was over, the gathering cheered loudly, and Rona, dressed again in her blue dress, smiled shyly and bowed. Helen bowed too and waved to Yann and the others up on the mound.

When they left the centre of the circle, the tall willowy woman took their place and started to tell how the northern islands were created, from stones thrown by ancient giants in battle. As Helen and Rona returned to the mound, there were fewer hostile faces in the crowd than before; some people and beasts smiled directly at Helen and even patted her on the back.

Before their friends could tell them what they thought of the performance, a red streak buzzed up to them and hovered just in front of Lavender.

It was a wizened little fairy in a dress made of poppy petals. She twittered to Lavender, "If I heard the Book's answers and that selkie song correctly, then you have been very busy lately, you and your great daft hulking friends." She waved her wand vaguely at the other fabled beasts, who all ducked. "But I *am* glad you got it right in the end. That is often – though not always – the only thing that matters."

Then she darted over to Helen and peered at her.

"So you are Lavender's human friend. She'll grow out of it eventually I'm sure, or you will. In the meantime, be welcome at our gatherings. If you keep our secrets, we will keep yours. Oh, and don't pester her for love potions or tinctures to get rid of spots. That's very tiresome." And she flew away.

Yann grunted. "They will all know in the end, won't they? But that song means we are already telling the story from our point of view. If you sing it often enough, Rona, then our version of foolish curiosity followed by bravery will be stronger than anyone else's accusations of stupidity or treachery."

Rona said to Helen, "I think Yann is right. We should play it together to our people when we can. Will you join me again in our quest song?"

"Of course, but I would also like to play it next week, Rona, at my school concert, because I need to play a piece I really care about, and this quest song is perfect for me. Do you mind if I just do the tune, without your voice?"

"You don't want me to go on stage with you in my seal self?" Rona tried to sound offended but then laughed. "Your human audience will never know what it's missing."

Yann sighed deeply as if all his questions had been answered, then settled on the ground, his legs bent under him. Lavender stayed perched on his shoulder, and Rona sat on the grass, leaning against Yann's flank.

Helen stood awkwardly nearby for a moment, then Sapphire growled a comment and took off towards the gathering.

"Do the dragons dance too?" Helen asked.

"No, they do a firework display," said Yann. "Please, sit down with us and watch."

Helen sat down beside Rona, leaning back on Yann's warm flank. Lavender dimmed the light balls around their heads as six dragons met in the sky above. It was not possible to see their colours in the dark but Helen thought Sapphire was probably the smallest one.

Suddenly, the dragons began to send arcs of sparks and flames into the darkness. There were no startling explosions like a human firework display, but a constant roar from the dragons' throats.

They created worlds of fire, globes, boxes and pyramids; they caught golden sparks in meshes and nets of flame; they made red-hot rubies and white-hot diamonds and strung necklaces with the stars.

Finally, they created a huge waterfall of rainbow flame falling towards the earth, which faded and went out only a hand-span above the watchers' heads.

The roaring stopped and the sky went dark. Still dazzled by the display, Helen heard a tapping noise behind her. Yet there was nothing there but Yann's warm ribcage ... and the pouch around his waist.

"Can you hear that?" she asked.

"Yes," said Yann, "Catesby's hatching already. Soon we will all be together again."

Read on for a sneak preview of
Helen's next adventure in

Wolf Notes
and
Other Musical Mishaps

Helen walked up to the boy with the dark red hair and the chestnut horse's body, whispering, "Hello, Yann."

"Healer's child!" The centaur's voice was sharp with surprise.

She glanced at the pale girl by his hooves. "Does your friend need my help?"

Rather than waiting for an answer, Helen slid her hands under one side of the bookcase. The centaur leant down as low as he could and grasped the other side. On his whispered count of three, they heaved the bookcase off the girl. She groaned, but didn't move.

They propped the empty bookcase between a flowery armchair and the wall, then started lifting books and sheet music off the girl.

The bookcase had been filled with printed music, but metronomes and music stands had also been piled onto its deep middle shelves.

After Helen and Yann had shifted the loose paper, they realized that a metal joint from a music stand had stabbed the girl in the upper arm. When she saw Helen staring at her, the girl bared her teeth in a growl, or possibly an attempt at a smile through the pain.

Helen knelt beside her. "I'm going to pull the metal out of your arm, then cover the wound, if you'll let me."

The girl looked up at Yann, who smiled reassuringly.

The metal spike had penetrated the girl's skin, but hadn't cut too deeply into her arm.

"Yann, hold her tight. This might hurt."

Yann's front legs knelt on the floor and he grasped the girl's shoulders. Helen put one hand on the girl's left elbow and with the other she steadily pulled the length of metal out of the girl's arm. The girl whimpered, once.

The wound started to overflow with blood. Helen opened the rucksack. She stemmed the bleeding with sterile swabs, then lifted the arm high, to slow the flow. "Hold it up for a minute, then I'll bandage it."

She kept her hand curled round the girl's elbow to take the arm's weight, then finally looked straight at Yann.

"What are *you* doing here?" they both whispered at once.

There was a moment's silence. Then they both spoke again.

"What are ...?"

Helen sighed. Yann scowled.

"You first," offered Helen.

"Me first," demanded Yann.

She grinned. He cleared his throat. "Your home in Clovenshaws is many miles away, to the south and east of these forests. What are you doing here?"

"I'm here for the music summer school; the one I was auditioning for when we met last winter. Professor Greenhill has rented the lodge for our school and, at the end of the week, we'll be performing nearby for a specially invited audience. You live miles from here too, Yann. Why are you here? Why have you and your friend broken into our rehearsal room?"

"I can't tell you why we are here, just that you must

leave. This is not a safe place for human children, especially ones so skilled in music. You must go. Now!"

"You've got to be kidding!" Helen's whisper cracked into a yell. The girl between them said softly, "How do you know this human child, Yann? Did you know she was here? Is that why you wouldn't let my brothers howl tonight; why you wanted me to be tame, just ripping drums and biting strings, rather than scaring the sleepers themselves?"

Helen twisted round to look at the shelves of instruments under the window. Two African djembes had rolled onto the floor, their drum skins torn open.

"Did you slash those drums?" Helen snapped.

The girl ignored her. "Who is this human, Yann, who speaks to you as if you were her friend and to me as if I were her dog?"

Yann said in a formal voice, "Let me introduce you. This is Helen Strang, the healer's daughter, who helped me and my friends when we fought the Master of the Maze last winter. She healed my leg, gave Sapphire back her sight, saved Lavender's life and answered many riddles. She is a friend to fabled beasts."

He gestured at the girl on the floor. "This is Sylvie ..."

"Don't tell her who I am!"

Yann smiled. "This is Sylvie Hunt, a shy friend of mine. I'm helping her defend the fabled beasts' territory in the West Highlands. But you won't be able to help us, healer's child, as your presence – and your music – will aid our enemies. So you must go."

"No! I'm not leaving until after the midsummer concert."

"You are leaving now, girl." Yann's voice was harsh. "Or we will drive you away."

"Why is this place so dangerous? Is the Master of the Maze here?"

"No, he has returned to his old labyrinth to heal his wounds and grow his hair. But here is a greater danger for a human child than even the Master. We can't tell you any more, as knowledge can draw humans towards the danger. I can only ask you to leave. Please, Helen."

Yann had never called Helen by her name before, not to her face.

"Please go home, Helen."

She acknowledged the offer of deeper friendship with a smile. "Thank you for caring about my safety, Yann. But my week at this summer school isn't about safety, or even about friendship. It's about music. This is a once in a lifetime chance to play the greatest music, with the greatest musicians. I'm not running away."

The girl on the floor laughed.

"They've enchanted her already! 'A once in a lifetime chance!'" she repeated sarcastically. "It would be a lifetime! Human girl, listen to your friend. If his gentle persuasion doesn't work, my brothers won't be so soft."

This time, she did growl.

Helen laid the bandaged arm in the girl's lap and looked at her thin face.

"What *are* you?" Helen asked bluntly.

"I'm Sylvie. Yann told you."

"He told me *who* you are. Hello, Sylvie. Nice to meet you, Sylvie. Now *what* are you? And why are you trying to drive me away?"

"Do you really want to know?" The girl's yellow eyes

narrowed, her lips drew back and her long teeth gleamed white in the light from the lacy lampshade above.

"Do you *really* want to know?"

Helen felt the hairs on the back of her neck bristle ...

To be continued ...

TIME TRAVEL TROUBLE

from Scottish Children's Book Award winner Janis Mackay

Time travel is a tricky business. From getting a lost girl back to *when* she came from, to finding lost title deeds when the world is on the verge of war, Saul and Agnes's time-twisting adventures could lead to a whole host of problems...

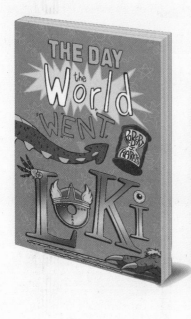

Lewis and Greg might have *accidentally* summoned Loki, the Norse god of mischief. Not to mention his hammer-wielding big brother Thor, who's trapped in the boys' garage… But it wasn't their fault!

With a gang of valkyries chasing them from St Andrews to Asgard, can the troublesome twosome outwit Loki and save the day?

discoverkelpies.co.uk

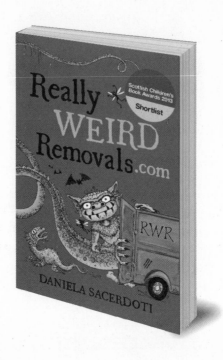

Mischievous fairies? Smelly troll? Werewolf snatching your sheep? Email the Really Weird Removals company!

Luca and Valentina's Uncle Alistair runs a pest control business. But he's not getting rid of rats. The Really Weird Removals Company catches supernatural creatures! When the children join Alistair's team they befriend a lonely ghost, rescue a stranded sea serpent, and trap a cat-eating troll.